Love From Sienna

Hope you enjoy
this story!
Love from
Joy Vee
xx

Love From Sienna

Joy Vee

BROAD PLACE
publishing

British Library Cataloguing-in-Publication Data.
A catalogue record for this book is available from the British
Library.

This book and all other Broad Place Publishing books are available
from Broad Place Publishing.

ISBN 978-1-915034-01-4

The author can be contacted via her website:
www.joyvee.org

Cover Design by Taylormade Creative. www.tcdesign.com.au

Books by Joy Vee

The Sienna Series

The Treasure Man

Love From Sienna

The 'Love from Sienna' Journal

The Kai Series

Kai – Born to be Super

Kai – Making it Count

For more information, visit joyvee.org

Dedication

To Lily,
Thank you for constantly asking
'What happened to Sienna's dad?'
This book wouldn't be here without you.

To Sienna,
Thank you for continuing to inspire me.
I love you!

Chapter 1

'Dinner's ready!'

Sienna was in her bedroom, doing her homework, when she heard Mum shout. She got up and raced downstairs. As she reached the hall, her two younger brothers, Jack and Theo, tumbled out of the living room, and she followed them into the kitchen.

'Mum, this smells lovely,' Sienna said as she sat down.

'It's just macaroni cheese.' Mum looked tired. 'It's nothing special.'

'Macaroni cheese is my favourite!' Jack said, with all the enthusiasm of a seven-year-old.

'Everything is your favourite. You just love food.' Sienna nudged her brother.

Jack looked at her and nodded seriously. 'Correct, ten points.'

'Jack, I think we need to cut down the amount of television you watch,' laughed Mum. 'You sound like you're on a quiz show.'

Jack nodded. 'Correct. Next question. What's wrong with that?'

Mum and Sienna giggled together, and Theo had to raise his voice to be heard.

'Thank You, Jesus, for this food. And thank You for Mummy and S'enna and Jack. Amen.'

'That was a lovely prayer, Theo.' Mum picked up her knife and fork. Sienna was grateful that Theo had only included the family in his prayers. One time, he'd thanked God for his entire nursery class. By the time they'd opened their eyes, the food was nearly cold, and Jack's plate was half-empty.

She looked around the table and felt happy. Then she felt a little niggle. As she looked at her family, full of smiles and conversation, she remembered their next-door neighbour, Mrs Smith, who lived on her own. Mrs Smith's dinner times would usually be quiet, not full of chatter and giggles like this.

'Mum, do you think we could invite Mrs Smith for dinner? It must be lonely to eat dinner on your own all the time.'

Mum slowly chewed her pasta.

'Yes, we could do that. Were you thinking of one time, or maybe having her over one day a week?'

'I think one day a week is better.' Jack spoke with his mouth full. 'Once she's tasted your delicious food, she'll find it hard to stay away!'

Sienna smiled.

'OK, but I'll need your help.' Mum put down her knife and fork. 'How about we invite Mrs Smith to come for dinner on Thursdays? Jack, in the morning, I'll need you to help Theo get dressed while I put everything in the slow cooker. Sienna, after school, I'll need you to set the table. If we all work together, we can do this.'

'And me. What's my job?' asked Theo.

'You have the hardest job. You need to ask Mrs Smith what her favourite food is. Can you do that?' Mum asked.

Theo nodded and grinned at her.

'After dinner, can I make an invitation and take it round to her?' asked Sienna.

'Of course, but go through the back gate between the gardens. It's easier than going to the front door. By the way, I'm working late tomorrow. Alison will pick you up.'

'Alison!' shouted the two boys.

Sienna bit her bottom lip. 'I hope she won't be late.'

Chapter 2

Sienna looked up and down the road again. There was no sign of anyone. The last of the parents and children had disappeared from After-School Club five minutes before. She looked back at her brother, Jack. He was pretending to be a tight-rope walker, trying to balance on a painted line on the ground. At eleven, she was old enough to walk home alone, but she knew school wouldn't let her take her little brother too.

'Sienna, Jack! Sorry I'm late. You wouldn't believe the day I've had.'

Jack looked up with a smile.

'Hi, Alison. That's OK.'

'I thought you'd forgotten us.' Sienna frowned slightly as Alison stopped to catch her breath.

'Alison'd never forget *us*.' Jack smiled. 'She might forget the time, but she wouldn't actually forget us – well, not *me*, anyway.'

'We need to hurry to get Theo,' Sienna said. 'His childminder doesn't like it when we're late.' Sienna hoped she wouldn't just put the three-year-old out on the street.

'Can you run?' asked Alison, as they all filed out of the school playground.

'Try to keep up!' Jack shot off. Sienna ran after him. A minute later, she realised Alison was getting left behind. Alison was their Sunday school teacher, they called it Kids' Church. But since meeting her three and a half years ago, she had become like part of the family. Sienna waited for her to catch up, linked arms with her, and the two of them walked together.

'So, tell me again, why is your mum working late today and all day tomorrow?'

'She said it was a stock-check. Everything in the shop must be taken off the shelves, counted and put back on again. They do it every year.'

'That's a big job!'

'Yes, other years Mum didn't have to stay late, because she had to look after us, but she's got a new boss now. He said it was her choice to have kids, and she should still do the work. He's so mean.'

'Wow! That's not fair.'

'That's not the worst thing.' Sienna was glad to have someone to talk to about it. 'He got rid of all the Saturday staff and is making everyone else do the work. Now Mum has to go to work two Saturdays a month. He's such an idiot.'

Sienna felt a little niggle inside, feeling bad about the strong words she'd said. But she pushed down the niggly feeling and kept walking.

'Sienna, you can't say that.' Alison's voice was firm, but kind.

'Why shouldn't I? He's keeping my mum from me, and now she's too tired to do anything fun on Sundays. She goes to church then sleeps on the sofa all afternoon.'

'I understand you're unhappy,' Alison said, 'but you have to be careful with your words and thoughts. It sounds like you are becoming bitter. Your mum may need to look for other work or write a letter to head office. But you calling the boss names isn't helping anyone.'

Sienna chewed on her bottom lip, wanting to change the subject.

'Maybe we can do something nice for your mum when we get home. Let's cook her favourite meal and make sure all your school uniforms are washed,' Alison said, waving at Jack as he waited outside the childminder's.

'Maybe we could strip the beds and clean the bathroom and wash the kitchen floor?' Sienna suggested.

Alison's eyes grew larger as she listened to everything on Sienna's list.

'I'm only looking after you one weekend. Do we have time?'

'Well, it's what Mum does every weekend, but if you aren't up for it...'

'No, no, we can do all of that! And when we've done the jobs, I'll take you all to the pond to feed the ducks.'

'Yay, duck pond!' Theo said, stepping out of the house as they walked up. The childminder glared at Alison, then looked at her watch.

'I'm so sorry,' said Alison. 'I'm not used to all this.' The door slammed firmly in her face.

'I really must try harder,' she muttered as she took Theo's hand. Looking up at Jack and Sienna, Alison smiled. 'Let's pop to the shop and buy something nice for your mum's dinner. What's her favourite?'

Chapter 3

'It's my birthday at the end of this month. Did you know, Alison?' Jack asked as they ate dinner around the table in the kitchen.

'I knew that. How old will you be?'

'I'm gonna be eight.' Jack pushed another chicken nugget into his mouth.

'When's my birthday? I want to be a big boy.' Theo folded his arms and frowned. Sienna thought he looked cute. From the way Alison's lips were wiggling, Sienna could see she was trying not to laugh.

'It'll be your birthday in the summer, then you'll be four!' Sienna tried to coax a smile out of her brother.

'Yes, but it's my birthday first,' Jack said, taking a nugget off Theo's plate and eating it. 'Mum said I can have all the special people in my life over for lunch. So, I want you and

Mrs Smith and Noah.' Suddenly Jack froze. He stopped talking. He even stopped chewing. It was like someone pressed 'pause'.

'Jack?' Alison leaned over and gently shook his arm. 'Are you OK?'

Finally, Jack took a deep breath. He looked up at Sienna. His eyes were big and sad. Sienna knew exactly what he was thinking.

'Theo, look, your plate's empty. Can you go upstairs and wash your hands?' Sienna made her voice sound bright and cheerful.

'S'enna come too.'

'No, you'll be four soon. You need to practise doing it on your own. Can you do that? Like a big boy?'

Theo nodded and scrambled off his chair. They heard him climb the stairs. Sienna looked back at Jack as he wiped a tear away with his shirt sleeve.

'What's wrong? You two are scaring me,' said Alison.

'Jack's fourth birthday was the last time we saw Dad,' Sienna said in a tiny voice. 'We had a party in a church hall. There were lots of people there. It was before we moved here. I remember Mum's brother, Uncle Matt, was there, and other neighbours and friends from nursery. There were bubbles and a bouncy castle. Dad and Mum were arguing before the party and didn't talk much when we were there.

17

We came home late, in a taxi, all of us. But in the morning Dad had gone. Mum was really upset and didn't want to talk about it. Soon after that, we moved here.'

Sienna looked at the table and was surprised to see blobs of water. She reached up and felt her face. It was wet. She hadn't realised she'd been crying.

'Every year I wonder if *this* birthday Dad will come back,' Jack said, looking up at Alison. 'Sometimes I think if we can get back to that place, the church hall, maybe he'll still be there, waiting for us to come and find him.'

Alison reached out and held both of their hands.

'That's really painful. I'm so sorry you guys went through that. Jack, I'm sorry that in the middle of your birthday, you have this big painful memory. It's very brave of you to share that with me.'

Jack took a deep breath and sat up straighter in his chair. 'I've got a few ideas about what might help make me feel better. The first one involves popcorn and a film. What do you think, Alison?' He gave her a wobbly smile. 'I'll choose the film; you can make the popcorn!'

Chapter 4

As Alison and the boys watched the film, Sienna kept thinking about Mum. Could she help Mum with the new boss? Maybe she could help her find a new job. She grabbed a large piece of paper from the cupboard and a few coloured pens. At the top of the page, she wrote: 'Top-Secret Mission: Rescue Mum from the Impossible Boss'.

Underneath, in a different colour, she drew a thought bubble with the words 'Find a New Job' inside. She decided that was the easiest one, but before exploring that, she drew more bubbles and wrote her crazier thoughts.

She wrote 'Win the Lottery' in one bubble, 'Marry a Millionaire' in another. In another bubble she wrote 'Sort out the Boss'. Remembering Alison's words from earlier, she drew a line coming out of the bubble and wrote 'Write a letter to head office'. That wasn't a bad suggestion. Certainly, it would be quicker than some of her other ideas.

Sienna picked up a different-coloured pen and thought of other jobs Mum could do. She thought about how great it would be if Mum only had to work when they were at school and they could have the holidays together. She thought about all the jobs at school and wrote a few down:

Lunch time coordinator
Secretary
Teaching assistant
School nurse

Maybe she could think about other jobs, not connected to school. What jobs paid well? If Mum could earn more money, maybe she could work fewer hours.

Sienna wrote:

Lawyer
TV presenter
Bridal designer

She looked at the other thought bubbles. She scribbled down a few more ideas and then sat back to watch the rest of the film.

Alison leaned over and looked at the poster. She picked up one of the coloured pens, and in the corner of the paper drew a little bubble. Inside she wrote the words: 'Forgive him'. Sienna scowled at Alison, but Alison just winked at her.

Chapter 5

The next day was bright and sunny. Sienna woke up early and heard Mum go downstairs to get her breakfast. She quickly got up and put on her dressing gown.

'Hi, Mum. You were home late last night.' Sienna came in the kitchen and gave her a hug. Mum looked tired but managed a smile.

'Hi, Pudding. Yes, it was a long day yesterday. But it was lovely to come home to my favourite dinner.'

'It was Alison's idea, but we helped her choose.' Sienna wondered if Mum would appreciate her 'Rescue Mum' poster. 'I've got something to show you.' Sienna ran into the living room and picked up the poster.

Back in the kitchen, she laid it out on the table. 'Here you go. Ideas to save you from your nasty new boss!'

Mum laughed as she sat down with her cup of tea and looked at the paper.

'Hmm, some of these are very interesting. Where do you suggest I find a millionaire?' she chuckled. 'What's this one in the corner, "Forgive him"? Sienna, that's very mature.'

'Oh.' Sienna shook her head. 'That was Alison's idea. Not her best, I think.'

'I'm not sure.' Mum tapped the corner of the paper slowly. 'I hadn't considered that option. It might be the best idea on here.'

Sienna tried not to be upset that Mum liked Alison's idea better than hers. Maybe she just hadn't read all her ideas properly yet.

Mum left for work shortly after Alison arrived, and they began 'Operation – Weekend Chores'.

Sienna stripped her bed, giggling as she heard Alison in the boys' room, shouting something about being a duvet monster and needing to eat bedclothes. The boys' laughter and shrieks echoed through the paper-thin walls.

By ten o'clock, all the jobs were done, and it was time to go to the duck pond. Just as they were about to leave the house, Alison popped back inside.

'Where are you going, Alison?' called Jack. 'Did you forget something?'

'I'm just grabbing some bread to feed the ducks.' Alison came out holding the remains of a loaf.

'Bread? No, Alison. No bread for the ducks – give them owwie tummy.' Theo explained, taking the loaf out of her hands and toddling back into the kitchen.

'When was the last time you fed the ducks, Alison?' asked Sienna.

'Years ago, when I was a kid. We always gave them bread.'

'Well, today's ducks are gluten-free. You have to buy them special duck seed,' Jack explained.

Alison burst out laughing. Sienna had never heard her laugh so loud.

'Oh, Jack, you are the funniest thing ever. I've never met anyone with a sense of humour like yours.'

Jack, Sienna and Theo, who was back from the kitchen, stood and looked at Alison. Jack tilted his head to one side and glanced at Sienna, who shrugged. The three children waited quietly for Alison to compose herself.

'You guys aren't laughing. Wait. Are you serious? Are ducks really gluten-free?' Alison wiped the tears from her face.

'I'm not sure about "gluten-free", but they can't eat bread.' Sienna explained. 'It's bad for them. We have to buy special duck seed. Jack wasn't joking.'

'Right,' said Alison, taking a deep breath. 'I'll get my money. Now I feel ancient.' She went back into the house, muttering. 'Ducks don't eat bread. What's next? Cats not drinking milk?'

Jack and Sienna looked at each other. Maybe that one could wait for another day. They didn't want to overwhelm Alison with all the ways the world had changed in the last few years.

Chapter 6

'Now I understand why you guys were so excited about feeding the ducks,' Alison said, giving them each a bag of duck seed. 'It's a special treat buying this duck seed. It cost more than ice-cream.'

'We usually share a bag, Alison. You didn't need to get us a bag each!' Sienna smiled her thanks.

'Well, now you'll have spare for another day.'

'Look at the ducks! They're so funny.' Jack started mimicking the ducks eating their food. Theo quickly caught on, and they both leaned their heads forward, with their arms tucked behind their backs, and pretended to scoop the little grains and seeds off the ground. The ducks quacked as though they were laughing at them. Alison grabbed Theo when it looked like he was going to topple into the water.

'Have you guys finished?' Alison asked.

'Nearly,' Jack said, picking up another handful of duck seed. Sienna noticed that Jack seemed to be throwing the food onto the ducks' backs rather than into the water.

Alison still wasn't happy and mumbled, 'What kind of world are we living in? This duck seed is too dirty, too grainy and too difficult to throw properly.'

After feeding the ducks and going back into the café to wash their hands, they headed to the children's play park, taking the leftover duck seed with them. They could come and feed the ducks again another day.

'Alison, it's Valentine's Day next Sunday,' Sienna said as they sat on the swings and watched the boys run around. 'We're not doing a craft, are we? I hate all that lovey-dovey stuff.'

Alison chuckled, pushing off with her feet and gently swinging. 'Me too. I can't stand the secret idea. "I love you – but not enough to tell you who I am"! Did I ever tell you about when I lived abroad?'

Sienna shook her head. She didn't really know much about Alison's life before they met her.

'I used to work in an international school, and on Valentine's Day, all my American kids bought me flowers and chocolates.'

'Why? Because you were the teacher?'

'No. They gave gifts and presents to people who were special to them. Every card was signed,' Alison winked, 'and said why they appreciated me and thanked me for being a friend. Those years in the international school were my best Valentine's Days ever.'

Sienna swung back and forth, thinking how great it would be to thank people who were important to her.

'Maybe we could do something like that. Change up Valentine's Day for Kids' Church. It could become our favourite day of the year, instead of one of the worst!' she suggested.

'What ideas do you have?'

'Well,' Sienna tipped her head on one side as she thought. 'We could make cards, but write special messages in them. Us older ones could help the little ones. We could make cookies and write "Thank you for being my friend!" in icing.'

Alison swung slowly. 'I think we can do more than that! Loving our friends is great, but can we go one step further? Can we do something really different and radical?'

Sienna felt excited. What they were discussing was already pretty radical. How could they improve on it?

'What do you mean?'

Alison continued to swing, nodding her head slowly.

'I've got a great idea, Sienna.' Alison stopped swinging and grinned. 'I think you're going to love Valentine's Day this year. Come on, let's see who can swing the highest!'

Chapter 7

'OK. Settle down, everyone. I need to tell you something that shook my world this week.' Alison winked at Sienna as the rest of the children in Kids' Church sat on the floor, and the chatter died down.

'Yesterday, I went to the park with Sienna, Jack and Theo. We fed the ducks. Now, when I was little – 100 years ago – we would feed the ducks our scraps of bread. We would just grab the crusts from the bread loaf and run off to the pond. We got rid of our scraps, the ducks were fed, and we had fun for free. Win, win, win!'

Mia, Sienna's best friend at Kids' Church, put her hand up. 'Alison, I don't mean to be rude, but bread isn't good for ducks. It leaves them bloated.'

Sienna watched Alison. Her lips were wiggling.

'Maybe we made our bread differently back in the olden days, but the ducks seemed to enjoy the bread we gave them. But when we went yesterday, we had to *buy* duck seed. With money. We had to pay!' Alison looked horrified. The children just nodded because paying for duck seed was normal for them. Alison shook her head and tried to continue.

'So, do you think the ducks were worried about how they were going to afford the really expensive duck seed?'

'No!' Noah shouted from where he sat next to Jack. 'Someone else pays. They just enjoy it.'

'Exactly, Noah! That's exactly what God told me. The ducks were happy with their food when I was a kid and it was free bread, and...'

Sienna noticed Mia frown, as if she were wondering how happy the ducks really were with the bloaty bread.

'And when everything changed, and the duck seed became expensive, the ducks didn't know about that. They just knew that they were getting better, healthier food.' Alison nodded at Mia, who finally smiled.

'It's the same with us and God.' Alison sat back, as though she had given them a nugget of truth. Sienna was confused. Looking round, she could see the other children also frowning.

'God gives us duck seed?' queried Jack.

'Am I the duck or is God the duck?' asked Noah.

Sienna raised her hand. 'Alison, could you explain what you mean?'

Alison grabbed her Bible. Sienna breathed a sigh of relief. For a moment, she'd thought Alison was in a strange world of her own.

'In Matthew, chapter 6, verses 25 and 26, it says:

> This is why I tell you not to worry about everyday life—whether you have enough food and drink, or enough clothes to wear. Isn't life more than food, and your body more than clothing? Look at the birds. They don't plant or harvest or store food in barns, for your heavenly Father feeds them. And aren't you far more valuable to him than they are?

Those ducks didn't care if the food cost me nothing or cost me more than a pair of jeans. They were fed. They trusted we'd bring them food, and they got food. They weren't begging people for a couple of quid to get their duck seed; they weren't in their nest chewing their webbed fingernails, wondering if anyone could afford the food that day. They just saw people at the riverbank and knew it was dinner time.'

'So, we're the ducks?' said Jack.

'And God gives us the feed – the right feed – the one that's good for us,' added Mia. 'But we don't have to worry about how much it costs.'

'Why? Why does God feed us? What did it say in the bit I read?' Alison asked. She read the verses again. Several hands shot up.

'He's our Father, and we're valuable to Him,' Noah said when Alison nodded at him.

'Like treasure?' asked Theo, and Alison smiled.

'Exactly like treasure,' she agreed. 'Your heavenly Father loves you, values you and will take care of your needs.' Alison looked over at Sienna. 'Even if your earthly father isn't here to do those things, God is. He has promised to look after you because you are valuable to Him.'

An angry question popped into Sienna's head, surprising her.

If God is able to look after us, why does Mum have to work so hard? Does that mean we aren't valuable?

Chapter 8

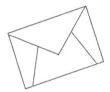

'Before we go, I have something for each of you.'

Sienna and Mia looked up. In her hand, Alison held a bulging bag.

'Oh, is it a present? I love presents!' Jack shouted.

'It's the best present you'll ever get,' smiled Alison. 'In this bag I've got a notebook for each of you.'

Sienna heard little groans from round the room.

'At the top of some pages of the notebook, I've written a verse from the Bible. A different verse on each page. And there are empty pages for you to write your own verses.' Alison continued as she began handing them round.

'One day this week, I want you to sit with this notebook, read the Bible verse and ask God what He is saying to you in this verse, then write your thoughts and ideas.'

Sienna flicked to the first page and saw that it wasn't an ordinary notebook. It was a bullet journal. It didn't have lines like a normal notebook; it had dots, so you could draw or write or do anything you want to. Sienna had seen some friends at school with bullet journals. They looked cool. On the first page, Alison had written the verse from class today:

> Look at the birds. They don't plant or harvest or store food in barns, for your heavenly Father feeds them. And aren't you far more valuable to him than they are?

'This notebook is not for me to mark or check what you have written. It is for you to talk honestly with God,' explained Alison. 'Ask questions if you don't understand something. Write prayers. Maybe the verse will encourage you to take action, and you can write what you did. But this is your space to engage with God and His Word.'

Jack put up his hand. 'Alison, do I have to write? Can I draw my thoughts? Sometimes that's easier.'

'Absolutely! You can draw, create your thoughts in Lego and take a picture, dance to it – whatever you want to do.'

There were a few gasps, and Sienna saw excited looks pass between her friends. Mia raised her hand.

'Alison, is it like memory verses? Do we have to learn the verses and get points for learning them?'

'No,' said Alison. 'You can memorise them if you want to, but I won't be checking. This is just for you to talk to God about the verse.'

Sienna frowned. 'So, if you won't be checking, and we can write whatever we want, what's the point?'

'It is really important that we learn Scripture. When we know verses from the Bible, God can remind us of those verses at just the right time and talk to us through them. But I want you guys to not just know the Bible in your head, I want you to live it. I don't just want it to be a list of words you remember, like a pop song or your eight times table. I want you to talk to God and learn to listen to Him.'

Alison looked around the room.

'If you have questions,' she continued, 'I want you to ask them, and have somewhere to write and remember the answer that God gives you. And to do that, we need to create space to think about His Word and listen to Him. I hope writing or drawing in this notebook will help the verses come alive to you.'

Sienna didn't quite understand why writing her thoughts would help, but Alison's ideas usually worked, and she was excited about using the bullet journal.

Sienna wrote her name inside the front cover of her journal so it wouldn't get mixed up with Jack and Theo's. She already had a question to write and wondered if God would give her the answer this week.

Chapter 9

Sienna decided Monday would be a good day to put into action 'Top-Secret Mission: Rescue Mum from the Impossible Boss.' She had created a plan which would let her try out quite a few ideas in one day.

'Mum, can I pop to the corner shop?' Sienna asked after they had dropped Theo off at the childminder's and listened to her complain about how late Alison was on Friday. 'I need a new pen for school.'

Mum frowned, glancing at the shop and down the road towards the school.

'I'll be really quick, and I'll catch you up. I've got some of my birthday money.'

Mum nodded, slowly.

Sienna shouted her thanks and ran down the road and into the little shop. Inside, she was pleased to see Mrs Khan behind the counter. Sienna liked Mrs Khan. She was always patient with the children, not letting grown-ups push in front of them.

There were a couple of other people in the shop, but no one else at the counter. Sienna knew she didn't have long.

'Excuse me, Mrs Khan.' Sienna gripped the edge of the counter and chewed on her bottom lip.

'Yes, honey?' smiled the older lady.

'Do you need any help in the shop? My mum needs a new job.'

'Really? Did she lose hers? Such a shame.' Mrs Khan tutted and shook her head.

'No, she didn't lose it. But she's working really hard, and she's always tired. I thought I'd help her get another one.' Sienna tried her sweetest smile.

'You are a wonderful daughter.' Mrs Khan leaned over and patted Sienna's hand. 'But I'm afraid I don't have any spare hours to give her, and if I did, I don't think it'd be enough. I'm afraid I can't help you.'

Mrs Khan muttered 'Such a good girl!' as she moved up the counter and served a customer buying a newspaper.

'Mrs Khan, can I buy a lottery ticket?' Sienna asked after the other customer had left. '

'Oh, sweet child!' Mrs Khan threw her head back and laughed. 'Winning the lottery is not a magic potion to solve all life's problems. I'm not sure those overnight millionaires are always happy in their fancy mansions over in Kensington and Chelsea. Personally, I don't think it's worth it. Anyway, I'm afraid I can't sell you a ticket. You need to be sixteen to play the lottery.'

'Oh, OK.' Sienna tried to smile, despite her disappointment.

Mrs Khan patted her hand again. 'I'm sure, with a daughter like you, your mum thinks she is the richest person in the world. You are a wonderful girl. Now, you need to hurry, or you'll be late for school.'

Sienna had to run all the way to school to catch up with Mum and Jack.

'Did you get a pen?' Mum asked.

'What?' Sienna had forgotten about the pen when talking to Mrs Khan. 'Oh, no. I didn't.'

'That's strange,' said Mum.

'We're going to be late! See you later.'

Sienna and Jack ran into the school playground before Mum could ask any more questions. But Sienna remembered what Mrs Khan had said about Kensington and Chelsea, and she already had another plan.

'Hi, Emily, are you OK? You look down.' Sienna noticed her friend sitting on a wall in the playground at break time.

'You don't want to know.' Emily played with a small corner of her pocket, fraying the edges.

'Try me.' Sienna sat down next to her.

'Dave's coming home tonight, so Mum has been cleaning all week. I feel like I never see her any more. She's either moaning because she's tired and Dave's away, or she's wrapped up with Dave when he's back.'

Sienna remembered that Emily's mum had remarried last year. She'd been jealous of Emily being a bridesmaid.

'Why's he away so much? Is it his work?'

'Yes,' Emily sniffed. 'He works offshore. On an oil rig,' she explained, seeing Sienna's confused face. 'So, he's away for three weeks, then home for three. When they first got married, I thought Mum and I would hang out while he was away, like we did before. But she just sits in the house, waiting for him to call. I keep telling her it's a mobile phone, she can take it with her if we go to the park or the shops. But she says she wouldn't want to talk to him when other people are around.'

Sienna nodded, knowing how boring it was staying at home when Mum was too tired or stressed to go out.

'But isn't it better having a stepdad than not having one? Didn't he buy you a new phone?'

'He did, and I'm glad Mum doesn't have to worry about money all the time, but I actually get sad when I see you and your mum talking on the way to and from school. You guys seem to be best friends. Mum and I were like that before, but now it's all changed.'

Sienna gave Emily a quick hug. She didn't know what to say and wondered if she should remove 'Marry a Millionaire' from the 'Top-Secret Mission' poster. But she had one last trick up her sleeve before she dismissed the idea totally.

Chapter 10

At lunch time, Sienna went to the school library and asked if she could use a computer. She had some important project work to do on the internet. After logging on, she searched for houses for sale for more than £5 million, in Kensington. Remembering what Mrs Khan had said about people living there in mansions, she wanted to check it out.

There were lots of very expensive houses for sale, and Sienna thought it might be a good idea to see if there were any parks nearby. She searched for parks near Kensington and found Kensington Gardens. It was near a tube station. If they went there for a picnic, and just bumped into a millionaire, who might want to marry Mum...

Sienna smiled, jotted down the information she needed, and hurried out to enjoy the rest of lunch time.

After school, Sienna found Mum sitting at the kitchen table with a cup of tea, looking at the poster. The spaghetti and bolognese sauce were bubbling on the hob, and it was Sienna's turn to lay the table.

'Are you feeling inspired?' she joked, pulling the plates out of the cupboard.

'Actually, I am. Your little poster has really helped me have a good day.'

'Which bit?' Sienna asked. 'Did you buy a lottery ticket?'

'No,' laughed Mum. 'It's this bit in the corner. "Forgive him". I've been thinking about it all day, and I tried it.'

'What? Why? Mum, your boss is awful. Why would you forgive him? He doesn't deserve it.'

Mum looked at Sienna and raised her eyebrows.

'Do any of us *deserve* forgiveness?' she asked quietly. 'I can think of plenty of times when I've messed up or upset people. But Jesus has forgiven me for all of it. That's what grace is. He forgives me for every wrong and hurtful thing I do, even though I don't deserve it. If He can forgive me for an entire lifetime of doing things wrong, surely I can forgive my boss for making me work on a Saturday.'

'But Mum,' Sienna put the plates down on the table and took a moment to sit down. 'You can't let him get away with it. How he's acting is wrong.'

'Yes, it is. By forgiving him, I'm not saying he isn't wrong. It just means that I'm no longer angry with him about it. When I say that I forgive him, I know he's wrong but I'm not allowing the anger I feel to grow into bitterness. I can do what he asks, or I can challenge him, without feeling resentful, and I can even pray for God to bless him.'

'Bless him?' Sienna was glad she was sitting, or she might've fallen over. 'How can you ask God to bless him?'

'That's the test for my heart. If I can ask God to bless him, and really mean it, I know I have no unforgiveness in my heart – and that's a good thing.'

'And you'd be happy if he got blessed, even though you're so tired?'

'Yes, Sienna, I would.' Mum drained her cup of tea and stood up. 'Especially if he was blessed with a promotion and a job in another branch.' She winked.

Chapter 11

On Wednesday evening, Sienna remembered that she hadn't looked at the bullet journal Alison had given her. While Mum was bathing the boys, Sienna settled down with her Bible, a pen and the journal.

Sienna read the verse at the top of the page.

> Look at the birds. They don't plant or harvest or store food in barns, for your heavenly Father feeds them. And aren't you far more valuable to him than they are?

She turned slightly so she could look out of the window. From where she was sitting, she could see the birdfeeder in Mrs Smith's garden. She watched the birds fly to the table, look around, grab some seed, and fly off. They didn't have to work or perform. The food was just there for them. She imagined all the work needed to plant fields, bring in the harvest, the enormous barns they stored it in. She'd watched programmes about farming on TV, and it looked like such hard work. But the birds didn't have to do any of that.

She used the dots on the journal to draw the window and then positioned the bird feeder in the middle. She tried to draw a couple of birds, but they weren't very good.

Sienna then thought about Mum going to work every day, having to work on weekends. 'And yet your heavenly Father feeds them. Are you not much more valuable than they?' For Mum, life wasn't easy like the birds. There was no magic 'bird table' for Mum that was replenished every day. Why did Mum have to work so hard?

Sienna wrote in the journal, under the picture of the window.

> *Why does Mum have to work so hard? Why isn't God looking after her? Doesn't God care about her? Doesn't He care about us? If it's true that we are valuable to God, why is it so hard?*

After writing this down, Sienna felt quite cross. She didn't want to pray; she didn't want to talk to God about being valuable. Her thoughts drifted back to last year and meeting a homeless man called Jamie. Theo had called him 'the Treasure Man'. He was valuable to God, but his life wasn't easy. Sienna had a niggly feeling God was trying to tell her something, but she didn't want to listen. She didn't want to remember Jamie. She wanted to think about Mum, and how unkind her new boss was and how difficult their lives were.

Pushing away her Bible and the journal, Sienna took the pen and went into the kitchen. On the table was the 'Top-Secret Mission' poster she'd made. It was time to update it.

She crossed out the bubble that said, 'Win the Lottery', remembering what Mrs Khan had said about the winners not always being happy.

Next to 'Marry a Millionaire,' she wrote 'Kensington Gardens. Picnic?'

Looking closer at the poster, she saw that someone else had updated it. Next to the bubble in the corner, someone – probably Mum – had written Colossians 3:13. Sienna was about to get her Bible and look it up when Mum called downstairs.

'Sienna, can you get Theo's toothbrush? I think I left it in the kitchen this morning.'

Sienna looked around, found the toothbrush, and ran upstairs. 'Maybe I can make up a bedtime story to tell Jack and Theo. I've got some great ideas!'

'Thanks, Sienna. That'd be great! It'll give me a chance to clean up this bathroom.'

Sienna looked at the bombsite that used to be their bathroom. 'I don't think my story will be *that* long!'

Chapter 12

'Are you working this Saturday?' Sienna asked over breakfast the next morning.

'No, not unless they call me in to cover someone who's ill. Why?'

'I was wondering if we could go for a picnic somewhere new. Explore a new place?'

'Sounds like a great idea. Did you have anywhere in mind?' asked Mum.

'I was wondering about Kensington Gardens.' Sienna tried to keep her voice light, as though she didn't care.

'Really?' Mum raised an eyebrow. 'But that's not a new place. We go there all the time.'

'Do we?'

'Yes. You know the play park with the big ship that you guys climb on? And the palace with the beautiful gardens.'

'Oh, is that Kensington Gardens?' Sienna wished she'd done her research better. 'I just thought it would be interesting.'

Mum's eyes flicked over to the poster, rolled up on the kitchen windowsill, and smiled.

'We can certainly go there on Saturday if the weather's good. Thanks for thinking of it, Sienna.'

At school that day, Sienna wondered whether she could go back to the library and research Kensington a little more. But when she got to the library at lunchtime, she saw Emily sat in a corner by the window, her shoulders sagging and her head down.

'You OK, Emily?' Sienna whispered. As she got nearer, she saw that her friend's eyes were red and puffy. Sienna wondered if she'd been crying.

'My mum's going to have a baby,' whispered Emily. She put her hands in front of her face and sobbed.

'But Emily, that's great news! Jack and Theo are my best friends. Having little brothers and sisters is amazing.'

'But your brothers are old enough to play with. You all grew up together. This baby will only be starting school when I'm sixteen.'

Sienna realised how different Emily's experience of being a big sister would be. There would be no playing together, having secrets and giggling, like she did with Jack and Theo.

'And I'll be left out.' Emily took her hands from her face and continued, fresh tears rolling down her cheek. 'Everyone else in my family will have Dave's surname, and I'll be on the outside with Dad's name.'

'Maybe you could change it to Dave's?' Sienna suggested. She was surprised when Emily glared at her.

'No. I love my name. It's mine. I don't want to change it. I didn't want Mum to change hers, either. Why couldn't Dave change his name to ours? There were two of us and only one of him.'

Sienna shrugged. It was a good argument. She knew she would feel weird if Mum had a different surname from her and her brothers.

'But a baby? Emily, that's lovely! You can sing to it. You have such a lovely voice. You can look after it. Imagine how happy he'll be to see you after school every day.'

'Or I could just feel even more on the outside. I hate having a step-dad.'

Sienna hugged her friend and wondered again if finding Mum a millionaire to marry would solve all their problems.

'Sophia's mum's about to have a baby.' Sienna remembered how sick her friend's mum had been at the beginning of her pregnancy. 'Why don't we go find her and talk to her? You guys could form a club: The Big Big Sisters' Club.' Emily smiled weakly.

'That could be fun,' she agreed.

'Great. Let's go find Sophia.' Sienna glanced at the computers and sighed. She wouldn't be able to do her research today.

Emily got up, pulled on her coat, linked arms with Sienna, and they went to find Sophia.

Chapter 13

Early Saturday morning, Sienna woke to the sound of rain drumming on her window. She got up and pulled back the curtains. It was torrential rain. There was no way they could go on a picnic today. Sienna thought she'd feel disappointed, but since talking to Emily the other day, she had been seriously rethinking the idea of Mum getting married again. Of course, it'd be nice to not worry about money, but Sienna liked her little family. The four of them were a team. She didn't want someone coming in and messing that up.

She checked the time. It was seven o'clock. Maybe she could start the day reading her Bible, like Mum did, and then make Mum a cup of tea.

She grabbed her Bible and the bullet journal and snuck downstairs. It was a little cold, and Sienna was glad she'd put on her warm dressing gown. In the kitchen, she put her

Bible on the table and quickly poured herself a glass of orange juice.

Opening the journal, she looked again at the verse written at the top of the page.

> Look at the birds. They don't plant or harvest or store food in barns, for your heavenly Father feeds them. And aren't you far more valuable to him than they are?

She looked at the picture and read the questions she'd written underneath about her mum. This time, instead of thinking about Mum, she thought about herself. She thought about the orange juice she was drinking. She hadn't had to work for that. It was provided for her. She thought about her snuggly warm dressing gown. Again, it had been given to her. Instead of thinking these things were just part of life, should she see them differently? Could they be gifts from a heavenly Father? Signs of His care for her?

'Are you not much more valuable than they?'

Sienna wrote in the journal:

> *Father, thank You for putting me in such a wonderful little family. Thank You I have everything I need. Thank You for the food we enjoy every day, and for my clothes.*

Sienna's eyes moved back up the page and remembered how hard Mum worked, especially with her new boss. But then she remembered last weekend, and the fun they'd had with Alison. The Saturday before that, they'd spent such an interesting time with Mrs Smith. She'd shown them old photos, and Jack and Theo had talked about it all week.

Thank You we have Alison and Mrs Smith in our lives. Thank You that even when Mum has to work, we can still have an amazing time with people who love us. Thank You for loving us so much. You gave us such amazing friends because we are so valuable to you.

Sienna sat back and reread everything she'd written. She felt peaceful and grateful. She found she wasn't angry any more with Mum's boss. She was thankful for all the time she had to spend with the special people in her life.

Sienna reached up and pulled the poster down from the windowsill. Unrolling it, she could see that other people had also been working on it. She recognised Jack's drawing. Next to the bubble called 'Sort out the Boss', he'd drawn himself as a superhero, using some kind of super-power on the boss. Beside it, in her small handwriting, Mum had written, 'Are you praying for him?' Jack had answered, 'Of course!' Sienna giggled, knowing that Jack hadn't meant that at all.

Next to the bubble marked 'Forgive him' there was the most writing. Mum had written more verses, and 'Pray a blessing on him'.

Sienna was excited to add to the poster. Near Jack's picture, there was still the idea to write a letter to head office, but Mum had also written, 'Refuse to work Saturdays. Legal rights?' Next to it, Sienna added, 'Thankful Mrs Smith and Alison can look after us!'

Sienna looked at the 'Marry a Millionaire' bubble. It looked like Theo had gone crazy here. There were scribblings that might be smiling faces and something that looked like a horse, but Sienna wasn't sure. There was box with round things underneath that could be a car.

Sienna wrote next to the bubble. 'Maybe not!' and copied down the Bible reference from her notebook. 'Matthew 6:25-26.' In small handwriting, she added, 'God gives us everything we need. We don't need a rich man.' Next to Theo's drawing she added, 'But a car would be nice!'

Sienna looked at the poster, pleased with her little family's ideas on how to help Mum. Then she remembered she wanted to make Mum a cup of tea and jumped up to put the kettle on.

Chapter 14

Jack and Theo didn't seem too upset when Mum announced they wouldn't be going on a picnic that day. They looked at each other with a secret smile. Sienna felt a little concerned.

'We'll make you a surprise,' Jack announced. 'It'll be really special, but you can't come into the living room for at least an hour!'

Sienna felt worried and looked at Mum. But Mum just smiled.

'Sienna, if we work hard, can we get all the chores done in an hour, so we can enjoy the boys' surprise together?'

Sienna thought for a moment about Emily. Since her mum had got married, they had a cleaner come in once a week. Now Emily didn't need to do any jobs. How nice would that be, to just lie-in on a Saturday, get up, meet friends, not do chores? Then Sienna remembered how upset

Emily had been in the library and how lonely she felt. Maybe she could look at this differently. This was a great opportunity to find out about Mum's family. She finished her drink and followed Mum upstairs to strip the beds.

'Mum, can you tell me about Uncle Matt? I remember him from Jack's birthday. But you never talk about him, and we never get Christmas cards.'

Mum laughed, pulling at a pillowcase. 'We're not that good at cards in our family! Usually the birthday presents – if we even got any – would come weeks or sometimes months after the actual day.'

Sienna giggled. Mum was still bad at remembering cards. One year, for her birthday, Alison had given her a box of cards, with a list of all her friends' birthdays stuck on the front. She'd spent ages finding out the information. Sienna thought it was a bit of rude gift, but Mum had loved it. Although, she was still late with Mrs Smith's birthday card the following week.

'Uncle Matt is an English teacher living in Poland. He teaches everyone – businesspeople, children, even a politician. I haven't seen him for a few years, not since Jack's fourth birthday. That's it, really.'

Sienna rolled her eyes. 'That's not it! Is he your big brother or little brother? Did you get on as kids?'

Mum sat down on the bed, looking out of the window. 'He was my little brother, about four years younger than me. The same as you and Jack. We got on really well. We were best friends. Sometimes I watch you with your brother and it's almost like watching my childhood all over again.'

'Was he funny, like Jack is?'

'Oh, yes. He had all these crazy ideas. If there was a simple way to do a task and a complicated, slightly dangerous way, Matt always chose the dangerous one. He'd call it the Creative Option. Sometimes I listen to Jack's wild ideas and I'm grateful that Matt isn't around. I'm scared of what they'd get up to if they were together in!'

Sienna laughed.

'Can you tell me a story from your childhood?' She asked.

Mum turned her head and wiped her eyes.

'I'll tell you what, Sienna.' Mum stood up quickly. 'You keep stripping the bed, I'll clean the bathroom, then we can both make the beds together. That should give Jack and Theo enough time to create their surprise.'

Before she could answer, Mum rushed out of the room, leaving Sienna holding a pillow and wondering what just happened.

Chapter 15

'Are you ready?' Mum knocked on the door, and Sienna heard some shuffling in the living room, before Jack solemnly announced, 'You can come in!'

Sienna and Mum opened the door and stepped inside. Something crunched under their feet. Sienna looked down, confused.

'Mummy, S'enna. It's raining, so we made a duck pond. We're ducks.'

Sienna looked around the room in horror and heard her mum gasp. Every bit of the floor was covered in duck seed.

'What have you done?' Sienna whispered. Mum covered her mouth with her hand and looked around with big, wide eyes.

'We've made a pond with the left-over duck seed Alison bought. Be really careful if you're coming in, it took us ages to get it all level.' Jack said from the other side of the room.

'Surprise!' said Theo, who was kneeling in the middle of the room with his hands tucked behind his back. 'Look, I'm a duck! Quack.'

Sienna watched as Theo leaned over and tried to pick up the duck seed from the floor with his mouth.

'I don't think you should eat that, Theo.' Mum's voice sounded very small. She coughed slightly. 'Jack, do you have the bags? I need to check what's in it.'

'It's alright Mummy,' Theo said, flapping his arms like wings. 'I'm gonna eat loads. I'm a greedy duck. Quack quack.'

He looked funny, and Sienna giggled. She glanced over at Mum, who was picking the duck seed bags out of the bin and trying to read them.

'Theo,' Mum's voice was serious. 'You need to stop eating, *now*!' Everyone froze and looked at Mum. Her face was pale, and she was staring at Theo. 'How much has he eaten?' she asked Jack.

'I don't think he's eaten any. I wouldn't let him till I heard you both come downstairs, although he might have sneaked a few bits while we were creating the pond.'

'Didn't you read it first? It's not for human consumption.' Mum's hands were clenched around the bags and her face was turning red.

'I don't know what those words mean,' Jack replied in a whisper, his eyes filling with tears.

Theo waddled over to his brother, still in his kneeling duck posture, and leaned against him.

'It's OK, Jack. I'm OK.' Getting no response from Jack, he looked over at Mum. 'I'm OK, Mummy.'

'I'm sorry. I just wanted to do something nice.' Jack's voice shook, and tears streamed down his face. Mum looked around the room, gave a deep sigh, then looked at the two boys huddled together across the room.

'It's OK.' She knelt in the duck seed and opened her arms. The two boys ran to give her a hug.

Sienna felt a little choked up but wasn't too sure if it was because everyone was hugging and crying, or because she knew it would take hours to clean up the mess.

And it did.

First, they swept the small bits up with a dustpan and brush, but more seemed to jump off the brush and away from the pan than into it. Then Mum vacuumed the floor, but soon the vacuum needed emptying. While she emptied it, Jack and Siena pushed the sofa and chairs into the middle of the room. The duck seed was everywhere.

It took two more times of vacuuming and emptying the vacuum cleaner before Mum was finally happy that they'd picked up as much of it as they could. Sienna wondered how three small half-full bags of duck seed could have produced so much dust and rubbish.

Just as they collapsed on to the sofa in a weary heap, an agonising scream ripped through the house.

Chapter 16

Hearing Theo's scream, Mum, Sienna and Jack shot off the sofa. They ran upstairs to the bedroom and found Theo on the floor, grasping his tummy and wailing.

Mum pulled her phone out of her pocket and gave it to Sienna.

'Call 999, tell them a three-year-old has eaten duck seed and is in agony. We don't have a car. We need help now.'

Sienna nodded and raced downstairs, dialling 999 as she ran. She ran into the kitchen and grabbed a pen and piece of paper, just in case. When the operator answered, she calmly requested 'Ambulance' and answered all the questions as clearly as she could. She was put on hold, and realised she was shaking. A little knock at the back door got her attention. She looked up and saw Mrs Smith, looking through the window. She unlocked the door to let her in.

'What happened? I heard a scream,' Mrs Smith said. For once, Sienna was grateful that the walls were so thin between their house and next door, and even more grateful for the little gate between the two back gardens.

'Theo ate duck seed. We don't know how much he ate, but he's screaming.' Sienna wiped away the tears that had fallen down her face while she'd been speaking to Mrs Smith.

'You're phoning the ambulance?' Mrs Smith asked.

Sienna nodded.

'Do you want me to stay with you?'

Sienna nodded again. She opened her mouth to speak, but a sob came out instead. Mrs Smith gave her a hug.

'You're doing fine. Hang in there,' she murmured.

'Hello?' Sienna needed to talk to the operator again, who asked some questions about Theo's colour and whether he had been sick. She didn't know and ran upstairs to ask Mum.

Theo was still screaming at the top of his lungs, but his face was deathly white. Sienna noticed Jack sitting in the corner, sobbing as he watched his little brother. She answered the operator's questions and gave the phone to Mum when she was asked for a grown-up. Sienna went over to Jack, took his hand, and led him out of the room.

'What have I done, Sienna?' Jack sobbed as she led him downstairs. 'He's in so much pain and it's all my fault.'

Mrs Smith was waiting for them at the bottom of the stairs.

'Now, now, young man. Come here.' The old lady wrapped Jack in a hug, and Sienna hurried back upstairs to help Mum.

The ambulance arrived within five minutes, but for Sienna, they were the longest five minutes of her life. At one point, Theo seemed to collapse like a rag doll. The silence was even more terrifying than the screaming. Mum and Sienna stared at him, watching to see if he was still breathing. But as soon as he took a breath, his eyes popped open, and the screaming began again.

They heard the ambulance siren in the street below. 'Run down and let them in, Sienna,' Mum said.

'It's OK, Mrs Smith is here. She'll let them in.' Even as she spoke, Sienna heard the door open and heavy steps on the staircase.

'Mrs Smith is here?' Mum seemed confused for a moment. As the paramedics came in and surrounded Theo, Mum looked around the room. She seemed lost. Sienna reached out and held her hand, which seemed to snap her out of her daze.

'Ask Mrs Smith to stay with you and Jack, and ring Alison too. I need to go with Theo. I'll call and let you know how he is, OK?'

Sienna nodded and quickly hugged Mum. They followed the paramedics and a screaming Theo out of the bedroom and down the stairs. Before she left, Mum turned and grabbed Jack and pulled him into a strong hug.

'This is not your fault!' Sienna heard her say. Mum pulled back and looked Jack in the eye. 'It's not your fault!' She repeated, before nodding to Mrs Smith and hurrying out of the house.

The door closed behind her, and silence filled the hallway. No one said anything. There didn't seem to be any words to say.

Chapter 17

'Maybe we should pray.' Sienna noticed how small her voice sounded. Jack sniffed and nodded. Sienna looked at Mrs Smith.

'Well, you kids know I don't really pray, not like you children do, but I think if ever there was a time to start, it's now,' Mrs Smith said, quietly.

'Dear Jesus...' Sienna found it more useful to keep her eyes open than close them. When she closed them, she could just see Theo screaming on the floor. 'We need You to help Theo. Please stop the pain, stop the duck seed from hurting him. Please, can he be OK? Amen.'

'Dear God...' Jack sniffed and wiped his nose with the back of his hand. 'I'm so sorry I let Theo eat the duck seed. Please make him better. I'm so sorry.' Sienna reached over and stroked Jack's back. His prayer finished with a big sob instead of an 'Amen', but Sienna knew that God didn't mind.

'Dear God, It's me, Barbara. It's been a while.' Mrs Smith coughed nervously before continuing. 'We haven't really spoken since I was the girl's age. But I'm talking to You now because it's important. Please look after that young 'un, and his mum. Please let him just, I don't know, be sick, or something. Anything to stop him from being in that pain. If You could do that, I'd be grateful. Thank You very much, and Amen.'

Sienna looked up at Mrs Smith and smiled at her.

'Now then.' Mrs Smith looked at the two children. 'Let's put the kettle on. Sienna, you call your friend Alison. I can stay with you till your mum gets back, but Alison's better at praying than I am, and this calls for the big guns.' Mrs Smith bustled through to the kitchen. Sienna went into the living room to call Alison, leaving Jack sitting alone on the stairs.

'Alison, is that you? Your voice sounds funny.'

'Sienna? I was asleep. What time is it? I'm not supposed to be looking after you guys, am I?'

'It's just past eleven. It's quite late. No, you aren't meant to be here, but I'm calling to ask you to come over.' Sienna heard her voice crack as she spoke. Alison must have heard it too, because she seemed wide awake when she asked the next question.

'What's happened, Sienna? Are you guys OK?'

'Theo's ill. Mum had to take him to hospital. Mrs Smith's here with us, but could you come too?'

'Of course. What happened? How is he ill?'

Sienna didn't want Alison to feel bad, since she was the one who'd bought the duck seed.

'I think he ate something,' Sienna said in a quiet voice.

'OK, I'm on my way. Tell Mrs Smith I'll be there as soon as I can. I'm praying for Theo and all of you, OK?'

Sienna nodded, then remembered she was on the phone, and Alison couldn't see a nod. But before she could say anything, Alison had said goodbye and hung up.

Sienna sat for a minute, looking at the silent phone. She could hear Mrs Smith in the kitchen. Why did grown-ups always make cups of tea? Did it really make everything better, or was it just something to do? Sienna couldn't count the number of times she had thrown away cups of tea that grown-ups had made for her, even though she kept telling them she didn't like it. Maybe she should try it and see.

The living room door opened, and Jack's face peered round. Sienna patted the seat next to her, and Jack came over and sat down. Sienna knew Jack was feeling bad, but she didn't know what to say. She squeezed his hand. He squeezed back, and they stayed like that for a couple of minutes, quietly holding hands. Sienna couldn't remember

71

holding Jack's hand before today. He'd always fought to get away.

Suddenly the phone in Sienna's hand rang, and the caller ID showed it was Mum.

Chapter 18

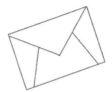

'Mum, how's Theo?' Sienna gasped into the phone.

'He's OK. Is Jack there? And Mrs Smith?' Just as Mum asked, Mrs Smith came into the room.

'Your mum?' she mouthed. Sienna nodded.

'Yes, we're all here. I'll put you on speaker.' Sienna pressed the button and Mum's voice filled the living room.

'Theo is fine, honestly! We got in the ambulance and drove down the road. He was still screaming, and the paramedics were trying to feel his stomach. We'd only got as far as the main road when Theo suddenly sat up, and was sick all over the ambulance, and me and everything.'

Jack pulled a face, and Sienna glanced at Mrs Smith, whose face had gone pale. She sat down heavily in a chair.

'He was sick about three times, then said, "All better now!" and fell asleep. He's still asleep now. I'm just waiting for the doctor to see him.'

'Are you sure he's asleep? And not unconscious?' called Mrs Smith.

'No, he's snoring away, and when I shake him, he says, "Mummy, duck seed's very bad!" and then starts snoring again.'

Sienna chuckled.

'So, being sick helped him? That's what Mrs Smith prayed.' Sienna said, looking at the old lady in the chair.

'Well, thank you, Mrs Smith! Your prayers worked! Now we just need to pray that we can get out of here soon.'

'I'll stay with the young 'uns and Alison's coming over too. So don't you worry,' Mrs Smith said.

'Thank you, I'd better go. I don't want Theo to wake up and me not be there.'

After a quick flurry of goodbyes, the phone went dead, and both children looked at Mrs Smith.

'Well, would you believe it? I'm so relieved he's OK. Who's for a cuppa?' Mrs Smith struggled to her feet.

'I'll have one, if you're making it,' a friendly voice said from the hall.

'Alison!' Sienna jumped up and ran to give her friend a hug. 'Theo's alright! He was sick, and now he's OK. He's sleeping.'

'That is a relief. I wonder what he ate.' Alison looked over Sienna's head. 'Jack, are you OK?'

'It's all my fault,' Jack whispered slowly, shaking his head and looking at the floor. 'I let him eat the duck seed.'

Alison moved quickly to the sofa and pulled Jack into a hug.

Mrs Smith stepped out of the living room, closing the door behind her, and herded Sienna into the kitchen.

'Let's give them a minute to talk,' she said. Sienna was desperate to listen to the conversation between Alison and Jack, but she decided that this was a good time to try a cup of tea.

It was later that afternoon when Mum and Theo came home. Mum looked tired, but Theo was a bundle of energy. He was full of stories of the doctors and nurses he'd met, and the strange sights and smells in the hospital.

After saying goodbye to Mrs Smith, Mum went upstairs to talk to Jack, who was still feeling bad.

Sienna and Alison went into the living room and sat down together on the sofa.

'I'm so sorry I bought you guys that duck seed,' Alison said.

'You didn't know the boys would create a duck pond with it and eat it.'

'Create a duck pond? What do you mean?'

Sienna told Alison all about the boys' 'surprise', since it was raining, and they couldn't go on their picnic. She talked about how long it had taken to clean it all up, and even after vacuuming three times, she still wasn't sure they'd got all of it.

'Is that some there?' Alison pointed to the floor between the curtains and the big armchair.

'Looks like it.' Sienna jumped up and tried to get it. It was difficult to reach, and in the end, Sienna climbed behind the chair and had to lie on the floor to grab it.

Just as her fingers were nearly touching the duck seed, the living room door opened. Sienna heard her mum's voice.

'Oh Alison, I was so scared. Just before he finally threw up, I had been about to message their dad.'

Sienna froze, replaying in her mind the words she'd just heard.

Chapter 19

Alison locked eyes with Sienna, laying on the floor behind the chair. For a moment, no one said anything. Sienna lay there, with her hand reaching out towards the duck seed, wondering if she'd heard correctly. Did Mum say that she'd been about to message their dad? Does she have his phone number? Or did she mean an email?

She heard Mum gasp, but it seemed to be from a long way away. She wanted to move but couldn't.

She watched as Alison got off the sofa and moved towards her. She felt the chair move, and Mum and Alison crouched down in front of her.

'"Message their dad"?' Sienna whispered. 'You have Dad's number?'

Mum and Alison quickly exchanged a glance, then looked back at Sienna.

Sienna stared at Alison. 'You knew?'

'Sienna, it's complicated,' Mum explained, but Sienna didn't want to hear it. She jumped to her feet and hurried out of the room, slamming the door behind her. She ran upstairs and threw herself onto her bed.

Sienna heard her bedroom door open and close again. She felt the bed dip as Mum sat down next to her. For a while, no one said anything.

'You have Dad's phone number?' Sienna asked in a little voice. 'Do you know where he lives?' she added, after a slight pause.

Mum sighed and picked at the edge of the duvet on the bed.

'I don't have his phone number, but I can send emails. That's what I was about to send. Your dad works a long way away...'

'Mum, that's what you always say.' Sienna sat up and shouted. She gasped for breath and tried to blink away the prickly feeling in her eyes. '"Your dad works a long way away. It's complicated." But I want to know more. Where does he work? On the moon? Why does he never write to us or send us cards or presents? What about when he isn't working? Why doesn't he come and see us then?'

Sienna had never shouted at her mum like that before. For a moment they stared at each other. Sienna watched a tear slide down her mum's face and she blinked away her own tears.

'Please don't tell me I'm too young to understand,' Sienna continued in a quieter voice. 'You always say that too. I'm not too young. I need to understand.'

Mum took a deep breath and sat up straighter.

'What do you remember about when Dad lived with us?' she asked.

'I remember being happy when I was little. We laughed and did lots of fun stuff together. You and me, and then Baby Jack, were at home and Dad worked hard, but always wanted to play in the evenings.' Sienna's tummy began to feel funny, like there were lots of spiders inside. 'But then things changed. Dad was at home, and you went to work. It wasn't so happy then. I remember lots of shouting.'

Mum sighed.

'Your dad lost his job and struggled to find a new one. He was unhappy being at home with the baby, and I was frustrated having to work all day, then do all the housework in the evenings. I was so tired, I told him to either find a job or leave. He left and got a job in the Middle East – a long way away.'

'Why didn't we stay in touch with him?'

'It was just so difficult. He worked long hours, and then there was the time difference.'

Sienna didn't think that was a good enough excuse. She looked at Mum and raised her eyebrows.

Mum turned red and picked at the duvet again.

'If I'm being honest, Sienna, I was too angry with him. You children were so upset that your dad wasn't around, and then he would never call when he promised, so the two of you got even more upset. I was so annoyed with him. I didn't want to hear about his new job, or his new life. It was easier to not try.'

Sienna nodded slowly. She tried to make sense of all the thoughts and questions in her head.

'I was wrong, Sienna. I know that now. I'm sorry.' Mum pulled Sienna into a hug. 'I know this is a lot for you to take in. I promise I'll be here to answer your questions about your dad whenever you're ready, and maybe you might want to write to him too.'

Chapter 20

Sienna rolled her eyes as she walked into Kids' Church. Alison said she hated all the lovey-dovey stuff, but there were heart-shaped balloons everywhere and in one corner was a huge tissue paper heart, filling the space from floor to ceiling.

'So, today is our favourite day of the year,' Alison called out, bouncing excitedly around the front of the hall. She laughed at the children's groans.

'But I want us to think about it a little differently today. I don't like the way we usually do it, the secret valentine, where no one knows if it's real or a joke.'

Alison told the children about her time in the international school, and the cards and gifts from her American students. She talked about how much more the comments meant because she knew who they were from.

'Last night, I dug out the cards and read them again. They are still special. A message that says "I love you" never gets old, never stops touching your heart. So, before we think about who we want to give a message to, I wanted us to remember an "I love you" message.'

Alison pointed to the big tissue paper heart in the corner.

'What do you think is behind the heart?'

Hands shot up all over the room. Alison pointed to Theo.

'Is it chocolate for us?'

Sienna smiled. Theo always seemed to equate chocolate with love.

'Does the heart show us how much you love us?' asked Mia, who Sienna noticed was sitting next to a new girl.

'It's the biggest love in the *world*,' said Noah, standing up and making a huge circle in front of him with his arms.

'OK, and who shall I give this love to?' asked Alison, sitting down on the edge of the stage.

'Give it to me. I was a big boy in hospital,' Theo said, his face so serious that Sienna nearly giggled.

'I've been really good this week,' another of the boys shouted. 'I scored a goal in football. I deserve whatever's behind the big heart.'

Alison nodded and listened carefully to the other answers. A couple more children gave good reasons why they deserved the mystery treat. Sienna noticed that Jack was very quiet.

'OK, help me understand. Some of you think you deserve what's behind the heart because you've been amazing this week?' Several children nodded eagerly. 'Some of you have been quite quiet, so I'm figuring you've not had such a good week, and you don't think you deserve it.'

Sienna noticed Jack look at the heart and then look down and pull at his shoelace. Maybe he was still feeling bad about the duck seed.

'Jack, would you like to see what's behind the heart?' Jack looked up, ignoring the moans around him.

'I wanted to be chosen to look. I've been so good this week,' whispered one of the little girls.

Alison's eyes never left Jack's.

'Jack,' she repeated. 'I want you to look behind the heart.'

Jack got up and slowly walked towards the heart. He stood in front of it, looking very small. The heart was huge.

'Just rip through it,' Alison said.

'Smash it!' Noah shouted, and a few of the other boys called out too.

Jack slowly reached out and pulled the paper. The tissue heart tore apart, revealing a large cross. Everyone gasped.

'The greatest love was given to us when we least deserved it. That is grace – God's forgiveness and love to us, when we are at our worst.' Alison's voice echoed around the quiet room. 'The Bible tells us in Romans 5 verse 8, that "God showed his great love for us by sending Christ to die for us while we were still sinners." Before we think about how we are going to show our love for other people, I want us to spend some time thinking about how much God loves us.'

One of the helpers picked up a guitar and began to sing. Sienna noticed that Jack went over and sat next to Alison. Even from the back of the room, she could see his shoulders shaking and knew he was crying. She quietly prayed that he would know God's love.

Chapter 21

After the songs, Alison called the group back together.

'Today, we can show love and grace to someone through our craft. So, you have a choice. You can write a card to someone you love, to let them know how special they are. That's fine. Or what about someone who thinks they don't deserve God's love? Perhaps you could write to them. This is the best love message. On the craft table, there are lots of sticky notes with verses about God's love, so if you don't know what to write, you can just copy or stick one of those in the card. But don't forget to sign your name!'

Sienna knew straight away who she wanted to send hers to. She worked hard on making a beautiful card and then wrote inside it.

Dear Dad,

This is Sienna. I just wanted you to know that I love you and I pray for you every day. And that Jesus loves you too. In the Bible, in John 3:16, it says, 'For this is how God loved the world: He gave his one and only son, so that everyone who believes in him will not perish but have eternal life.'

We now believe in God, like it says in the Bible. Every day I pray you will find Him too.

My address is at the bottom of the card, and I'd love it if you wrote back.

I miss you.

Love from

Sienna

Sienna sat back and read her card. She was pleased with it and prayed that her dad would get it quickly and would like it. She put it in an envelope and popped it in her bag so she could ask Mum for the address later.

'Are you Sienna?' a quiet voice asked. Sienna turned and saw the new girl who had been sitting with Mia. She was a little younger than Sienna, nearer Jack's age.

'Yes, I'm Sienna.' She was still thinking about the card for her dad and forgot to smile. The younger girl shuffled her feet and frowned slightly.

'My name's Zoe,' she said. 'We've just moved here. I remembered some verses I learnt last year, I felt God wanted you to read them too. So, I wrote them in a card for you. I hope that's OK.'

Zoe held out an envelope decorated with stickers. Sienna looked at the envelope, then back at Zoe. It must have taken real guts for her to give a card to someone she didn't know. Sienna smiled.

'Thanks, that's really kind of you.'

Zoe nodded and skipped away to where Mia was helping the younger children write in their cards.

Sienna looked at the card and smiled. She put it in her bag to open later.

After lunch, Sienna told Mum about Kids' Church.

'We had to make cards for people who needed to know Jesus loved them. I made a card for Dad.'

Mum looked up from washing the dishes, her eyes wide.

'Oh, I didn't think you'd write to him so soon.'

'Is that a problem?' Sienna asked, watching Mum closely.

'No.' Mum hesitated. 'But I don't think we'll be able to send the card to him.'

'Why not? Don't you have his address?'

'Not really. He lives in a very strict country and there are lots of rules about how you can live, what you can and can't do, and the mail you can receive.'

'It sounds awful. Couldn't he get a job somewhere else?'

Mum shrugged. 'I don't know. But we can't post cards to him with Bible verses on.

Sienna frowned. After spending so much time on the card, she didn't want it to be wasted.

'I have an idea.' Mum emptied the washing-up bowl. 'How about I email your dad and find out how secure his network is? Maybe I can take a picture of your card and email that to him.'

Sienna nodded. It wasn't the same, but it was better than Dad not getting the card at all.

'Do you think he'll answer me?' Sienna concentrated on the plate she was drying.

'I hope so.'

Chapter 22

'You seem happier this morning,' Mum said to Jack, who looked like he was trying to win the world record for eating breakfast in the fastest time ever. He stopped, his spoon paused halfway to his mouth, and nodded.

'We're best friends again,' Theo explained, smiling up at Jack. Jack grinned back.

'What happened?' Sienna asked Jack. 'You were so cross with yourself about the duck seed, you stopped being Jack.'

'Yesterday, at Kids' Church, when I saw the big heart, I thought, "Oh, I was bad – I hurt Theo. That heart can't be for me." Then Alison asked me to see what was behind. I felt like I didn't deserve any love. But when I saw the cross, I remembered those words of Jesus - remember, Mum?'

Mum nodded. 'It was your memory verse last Easter. Luke 23:34. Can you still remember? That was nearly a year ago.'

Jack rolled his eyes. 'Of course I can. Jesus was on the cross and He looked at all the people who'd hurt Him and said, "Father, forgive them, for they do not know what they are doing." And I thought of me, not knowing what I was doing when I let Theo eat duck seed, and I imagined Jesus asking the Father to forgive me.'

'Wow,' said Sienna. 'That must've felt pretty good.'

Jack shrugged, like it wasn't a big deal. But the smile on his face told Sienna that he was feeling much better.

'That makes me think about my boss.' Mum put down her piece of toast and looked at Jack. 'Maybe he doesn't know what he's doing. Maybe he's so focused on getting the shop to work properly and earn money that he doesn't know how difficult it is for the rest of us.'

'So, do you just forgive him and let him get on with it, or do you talk to him?' Sienna asked.

'Maybe both. I've forgiven him, so I'm not angry, and now, maybe I need to talk to him.' Mum picked up her toast and gazed into space as she ate it, as though she were thinking through the options.

Jack watched her for a moment, and then shuddered, as though he'd had a terrible thought. 'I don't think I like growing up – the problems are too big,' he said, finishing the last of his cereal.

'Sienna,' Mum popped her head around Sienna's door that evening. 'I just wanted you to know, I've emailed your dad, and I'm waiting to hear from him. It can sometimes take him a couple of days to reply.'

'Did you email pictures of my card?'

'No, I asked if it was OK to send him pictures from you, if they had religious words on.'

'Why would that be a problem?'

Mum came in and sat on the edge of the bed.

'In some countries, it is illegal to be a Christian or to own a Bible. People who live in those countries need to be extra careful. I don't want your dad to get into any trouble.'

Sienna nodded. She wondered what it would be like to live in a country where it was illegal to be a Christian.

'I'm glad we don't live in a country like that.' Sienna snuggled down and pulled her duvet around her.

'Maybe we could pray for kids your age who live there and believe in Jesus. I'm sure they don't have an easy life.'

Sienna closed her eyes, and they prayed together for children living in those faraway places.

Chapter 23

Sienna was setting the table for five people when she heard a light knock on the back door. Mrs Smith popped her head inside and sniffed.

'Something smells good!' she said.

'We've made your favourite today, Mrs Smith. Sausage casserole.'

'You didn't let young Jack near it, did you? Don't want to be finding a bit of duck seed in my dinner.' Mrs Smith chuckled at the joke she repeated every time she popped in.

Sienna tried not to roll her eyes.

The door opened, and Jack and Theo burst in, full of news and amazing ideas. The closer it got to Jack's birthday, the more elaborate the ideas seemed to become. Sienna tried not to laugh as today's plans seemed to be circus-themed and involved Theo swinging down from the bedroom window on a rope, dressed as a ringmaster. Mum followed the boys into the kitchen.

'Do we need to be worried, Mum?' whispered Sienna, as Jack's next idea seemed to involve a flame-thrower.

'I'm not sure,' Mum replied, winking at Sienna. 'Thank you for your amazing ideas, Jack. I'm thinking cheese sandwiches and a game of Twister will be enough for your birthday party.'

Jack pulled a face, before suddenly adding 'What would be fun is if you change the body parts on Twister, so instead of hands and feet, it's elbows, knees and ears!'

'I don't know about more fun, but it'd certainly make the game shorter,' agreed Mum. 'I want to tell you about my day.'

Everyone turned to Mum, and Sienna suddenly noticed how tired she looked. Her face was very pale, and she had dark circles around her eyes.

'Some of the other people at work were sick of the new boss making them work on Saturdays. They all decided no one would go to work this Saturday. Everyone booked it off as a holiday on the calendar.'

Sienna gasped. 'Even you?'

'Well, I had already asked for that Saturday, and the one after it, off. It's Jack's birthday the second Saturday, and I need at least one full day to get everything prepared. But everyone else wrote their names on the holiday calendar, and when the boss looked at the rota, there was no one to work on Saturday.'

'Was he angry?' asked Jack.

'He was livid,' Mum explained, her eyes wide. 'He called each of us in and asked what we were doing and why we couldn't work. I explained it was Jack's birthday, and he said I didn't need an extra week to prepare, so I could work this Saturday and have next Saturday off.'

'That's not fair,' Sienna couldn't stop shouting out, although she knew it was rude. 'You've worked so many Saturdays. Although obviously we love it when you look after us, Mrs Smith!' She hoped she hadn't offended the older lady.

'No, I agree. You are good children, but looking after you all day is quite tiring. Sometimes I wonder if your mum works Saturdays to have a break from you all.' Mrs Smith muttered, shaking her head and spearing another piece of sausage on her plate.

'Oh no. I'd rather be with the children than at work on a Saturday,' Mum said. 'Anyway, I quickly prayed, and asked God for help. Straightway, in my head, I saw lots of numbers, adding up really quickly. It was strange.'

Jack laughed. 'That must be God! Mum doesn't like numbers. She's rubbish at maths. She has to ask me for help all the time.'

Mum looked at Jack and raised her eyebrows.

'Sorry! I didn't mean rubbish. I just meant that maybe it wasn't your favourite.' Jack desperately tried to backtrack.

'You're in trouble!' Theo whispered loudly. Sienna tried hard not to laugh.

'Anyway,' Mum continued, shaking her head slightly at Jack. 'It was like I could suddenly see all the hours I'd worked over the last few months, since the new boss arrived. I wrote the hours down and was surprised to see how many there were. I then asked the boss if he knew how many hours were on my contract, and what extra I needed to be paid for all this overtime.'

Mrs Smith hooted with laughter, leaning back in her chair. Sienna wasn't sure why she was laughing. She looked at Jack and saw he didn't understand either.

Mum looked at their confused faces and explained. 'If I work my normal hours – the hours on my contract – I get my normal pay. But if I work more than the hours on my contract, they pay me a lot more. Because I've been working so many Saturdays, he now has to pay me a lot more money. It was cheaper when he had the Saturday staff working. They have a smaller wage than I do.'

'So, you told him he needed to pay you more money?' Sienna checked.

'Yes. *Politely*. I said it politely.' Mum glanced at Jack.

'What did he do?' Mrs Smith asked, her face still red from laughing so much.

'He got on the phone to all the Saturday staff, apologised and offered them their jobs back. Not all of them wanted to return, but there will be enough to manage the shop.'

Everyone cheered.

'Does that mean we don't need our poster any more?' Sienna nodded towards the poster, rolled up on the windowsill.

'Let's keep it for a couple more weeks, just in case.' Mum winked. 'And I've really enjoyed seeing all your ideas appear on the poster. I think I'll miss it when it's gone.'

'Maybe we can make a new poster: Operation Jack's Best Birthday Ever!' Jack suggested.

'Hmm,' said Mum. 'We'll see.'

Chapter 24

Sienna woke up early on Friday morning. She looked across at her Bible and bullet journal and decided to read another of the verses Alison had written. She sat in bed, with her back against the headboard and the duvet pulled up around her. She opened the notebook and read the verse on the next page. It was from Isaiah 49, verses 15-16.

> Can a mother forget her nursing child?
> Can she feel no love for the child she has borne?
> But even if that were possible,
> I would not forget you!
> See, I have written your name on the palms of my hands.

Sienna read the words over again and again. They almost made her want to cry. She pictured Mum working so hard for them all, taking time to talk to them, teach them, encourage them. Mum loved them so much. She'd never forget them. And that's how God loved her.

She read the last line again. 'See, I have written your name on the palms of my hands.' She looked at the palms of her hands and imagined her name written on them. Then she imagined Jesus' hands. She thought of the nails that pierced Jesus' hands. These were signs of His great love for her.

'Thank You, Jesus. Thank You, Jesus, for loving me that much, and never forgetting me,' Sienna whispered.

She didn't feel able to write any words in the notebook, but drew a picture of Jesus's hand, with the scars from the nails. It made her feel so grateful.

The Bible verse about a mother not forgetting her baby made Sienna wonder about dads. Could a dad forget his child?

That afternoon, Mrs Smith was coming out of her front door as Sienna arrived home from After-School Club.

'Your mum told me you've been talking about your dad,' Mrs Smith said.

Sienna nodded, glancing round to make sure the boys were out of ear shot.

'Did I ever tell you about my dad?' Mrs Smith asked quietly. Sienna had never heard Mrs Smith mention her dad before. Sometimes she talked about her mum, but never her dad.

Mum and the boys opened the gate and tumbled up the path. Mrs Smith looked at Mum.

'Is it OK if Sienna comes with me to the shop? I need help to carry things.'

'Of course, no problem. We can all come if you like.'

'No, we'll manage fine on our own. We need to talk.'

Mum raised her eyebrows, glancing quickly from Sienna to Mrs Smith. She nodded slightly and smiled at Sienna as she walked past her into the house.

Sienna walked next to Mrs Smith, who didn't seem to be in any hurry. She didn't know if she should ask questions, so stayed quiet until Mrs Smith spoke.

'My father fought in the war. They sent him to France.'

Sienna had been studying the Second World War at school and knew that it hadn't been easy for any of the soldiers.

'I was only a baby when he left. I don't remember him before the war, but Mother told me what he was like. He used to be full of life, a big, joking man, always had a kind word. He'd give away his bus money to someone who looked like they needed it, even if he had to walk miles home.'

Sienna smiled, imagining such a warm-hearted man.

'But that's not the man we knew.' Mrs Smith stopped walking, and looked around her, as if she were looking at pictures from long ago, not the trees and houses around them.

'All I remember of my father growing up was an angry man, sitting in the corner. He'd shout at Mother to bring his paper, bring his tea, make his dinner. Us kids were frightened of him. We didn't stay in the house much. It was better to be out on the streets, even in the rain, than to be in the house with him.'

'That sounds awful. I'm sorry you had such a cruel dad.'

'You don't understand.' Mrs Smith looked at Sienna. Her eyes were red and watery. 'I didn't understand, either. He wasn't cruel. He was damaged. The war had broken him. He was angry about all the bad things he'd seen. Things we could never imagine. But mostly he was frightened for us, that we'd have to fight in a war like that one, and he couldn't stand the thought of it.'

Mrs Smith looked up at the sky, and a tear rolled down her cheek.

'He died when I was fifteen. His last words to Mother were: "Keep the children safe." We were the most important thing in his life, but he didn't know how to love us. He was too broken to be the father we needed him to be, the father he wanted to be.'

Mrs Smith looked at Sienna.

'I didn't understand all this till I was much older. I just thought my father didn't love us, didn't even like us. As you grow up, you see things differently. Your dad out there, maybe he's broken too. I don't know. Maybe he wants to be a good dad, but he can't. But it's not your fault. It's not that he doesn't love you. Maybe he doesn't know how to.'

Mrs Smith turned and kept walking down the street. Sienna's thoughts were all jumbled up inside her head, but the biggest feeling was sadness. For Mrs Smith and for her father. Loving each other, but not being able to feel that love.

Sienna jogged to catch up with Mrs Smith, then did something she'd never done before. She took Mrs Smith's hand. Mrs Smith kept walking, looking straight ahead, but Sienna felt her squeeze her hand.

Chapter 25

On Saturday, Sienna got up early and was surprised to find Jack already downstairs. He had a large piece of paper laid out on the kitchen table and was busy planning his party.

Sienna looked over his shoulder. Maybe the circus theme had gone too far. That drawing looked like a lion. And was that a knife-thrower?

Mum came into the kitchen and put the kettle on before examining Jack's poster.

'I need to pop into town today. Sienna, I'm dropping the boys off at Alison's on the way. Do you want to stay with them, or come with me?'

'Can I come with you? I love shopping.'

After breakfast, Sienna ran upstairs to grab her bag. When she picked it up, it felt heavier on one side. Opening it, she saw an envelope covered in stickers. Sienna remembered the new girl in church who'd given her the card on Valentine's Day.

Sienna sat on her bed and pulled out the card. Inside there were three words, and next to each word was a Bible verse. At the bottom, the new girl had written:

I hope these words help you as much as they helped me. A friend gave them to me last year.

Love from Zoe.

Sienna looked at the words.

Forgiven.
Forgive.
Bless.

She grabbed her bullet journal and flicked through it, looking for a page without a verse on the top. She soon found one and wrote Zoe's words and the verses.

Next to the word 'Forgiven' was the Bible verse Psalm 65:3. Sienna quickly turned to it in her Bible. Psalms were easy to find. They were right in the middle of the book. Sienna copied it into her journal:

> Though we are overwhelmed by our sins, you forgive them all.

She smiled. It was good to know that she was forgiven, no matter how many times she did things wrong.

The word 'Forgive' was followed by Colossians 3:13. It took Sienna a few minutes to find that one. She had to look at the contents page in the front of the Bible. Colossians was near the end of the book. She turned to the verse, hoping it was the right one. As soon as she read it, she knew it was.

> Make allowance for each other's faults and forgive anyone who offends you. Remember, the Lord forgave you, so you must forgive others.

Yes, that was clear. The last word, 'Bless' was followed by Luke 6:28. Luke was quite a big book. Sienna slowly flicked back in her Bible and found it.

> Bless those who curse you. Pray for those who hurt you.

After writing the verses, she wrote a question: *Who do I need to forgive?*

For a second her mind went blank, then she began to think of people. The first was Mum's boss. She was angry with him for treating Mum badly and making her work for so many hours. Even though Mum had sorted that out, Sienna still felt angry with the boss. She knew in her heart she needed to forgive him.

Next, she wrote 'Mum' in tiny letters. She was very upset with Mum for not telling them more about Dad and helping him stay in touch with them.

She wrote 'Dad' at the end of the list.

She looked at the list of names and the words and verses above them and felt a little lost with all the big feelings inside her. Maybe someone could help her with this.

'Dear Jesus,' Sienna quickly prayed. 'Please send someone to help me pray about these things. Amen.'

She pushed the card and the notebook into her bag and hurried to get dressed.

Chapter 26

Shopping was much faster without two little boys. Mum and Sienna really enjoyed their time together. After a couple of hours, they had picked up everything they needed for Jack's party.

'How about grabbing a drink and a sit-down?' suggested Mum, pointing to a small café next to the florist.

'I think we deserve it,' Sienna agreed.

They chose a little table at the back of the café, and Sienna listened in to nearby conversations as Mum went get the drinks.

'How're things at work?' she asked, trying to sound grown-up, as Mum sat down with their order.

Mum took a quick sip of her tea.

'That's better,' she smiled, sitting back. 'It's quite sad, really. The new boss got into enormous trouble. Because we had all been working longer than our contracted hours, he'd spent too much money paying us for our overtime.'

'But isn't it good that he got told off? He'd been really unfair to you.'

Mum tilted her head to one side for a moment.

'If you'd asked me that a month ago, I'd have said yes. I would've been thrilled that he was in trouble and maybe even doing a little happy dance.'

Sienna nearly choked on her milkshake, imagining Mum dancing.

'But when I read your poster, and the little bubble that said, "Forgive him", I knew that was a better way.'

'Why does it make such a difference to just say "I forgive you"? They aren't magic words.'

'No, but in a way, they are.' Mum knitted her eyebrows together and stared at her cup of tea. Sienna waited, knowing that whatever Mum said next would be worth the wait.

'Being angry with someone is like... eating duck seed.'

'What do you mean?' asked Sienna, surprised.

'Well,' said Mum. 'It really hurts inside. It doesn't hurt the person who made me angry – they don't care. It hurts me. The anger is inside me, and it's poisoning me.'

Sienna knew about anger inside, and how much it made her want to scream. She leaned forward, hoping that Mum's words would help her with those feelings.

'When I choose to forgive someone, it gets the badness out, so it can't hurt me any more.'

'Like Theo being sick?' suggested Sienna.

'Just like that.' Mum screwed up her nose.

'And do you feel better straight away? Like Theo did?'

'Not always,' Mum said. 'Sometimes the anger is very deep, or the hurt continues, and you need to forgive again and again. Sometimes lots of times. But we are always asking Jesus to help us forgive and remembering how much He forgave us.'

Sienna thought about Mum's words as she took a long slurp of milkshake.

'OK. Here's a question. If you'd forgiven him, why did you point out that he wasn't paying you right? Why didn't you just go to work when he asked you, because you'd forgiven him?'

Mum looked Sienna in the eye.

'When I forgive someone, that deals with my heart. But if their behaviour continues to be wrong and hurtful, that still needs to be addressed and stopped. Just because I forgive someone doesn't mean I will let them continue treating me badly.'

'This is quite a grown-up thing. I don't know if I understand it all.' Sienna shook her head.

'I'm still learning,' Mum said. 'I know I don't have all the answers.' Mum poured herself another cup of tea and took a deep breath. 'So, are we ready for Jack's party?'

Chapter 27

'These are for you!' Sienna held an enormous bunch of flowers out under Alison's nose as she opened the door. 'Thank you for looking after the boys!'

Alison laughed. 'We had fun, didn't we, boys?'

'We went to the park,' said Theo.

'And hunted for squirrels.' Jack commando-crawled down the corridor. Sienna could tell from how dirty both boys were that they had probably been doing that in the park, too.

'You must be exhausted,' Mum said. 'Thanks so much!'

'Anytime. Listen, I know you've been shopping all morning, Sienna, but do you fancy going for a walk by the canal? I'd like to hang out for a bit.'

Sienna looked at Mum, who nodded.

Five minutes later, everyone trooped out of the door. Mum and the boys headed home, and Sienna and Alison turned towards the canal. As they walked down the street, they could hear Jack asking Mum if she'd brought a ring-master uniform and juggling skittles he could set on fire.

'I'm almost scared to go to this birthday party,' Alison said. 'Jack told me about his poster. It sounds pretty full-on.'

'I wouldn't worry too much. We didn't buy anything dangerous. I just hope he isn't too disappointed.'

'You know, Sienna. I was praying for you this morning, and I felt like we needed to spend some time together. Is there anything on your mind you want to talk about or pray about?'

'Really? Wow! I just praying this morning and asked God to send someone to help me. Did He really tell you that this morning?'

'Yes, He did. So, what can I help with you with?'

'On Valentine's Day, I wrote a letter to my dad. I told him about God loving him and us praying for him. Mum said there might be some problems sending a picture of my card, because it had a Bible verse in it. But I really want to hear from him.'

Sienna wondered if Alison would try to give sensible grown-up advice, but she didn't. She stayed quiet.

'I'm afraid he's forgotten me or doesn't want to have anything to do with me,' said Sienna after a minute.

They walked along the canal in silence.

'I think God's asking me to forgive him. I don't want to be angry with him, but it hurts very much.'

Alison wrapped her arm around Sienna's shoulders as they walked.

'Yes, it does hurt,' she whispered, and they walked in silence for another couple of minutes.

'Zoe, the new girl, gave me a card.' Sienna reached into her bag and pulled out the card. She gave it to Alison, who pointed to a bench just ahead of them. They sat down.

Alison looked at the card, reading the words and the verse references.

'Do you know what these verses say?' she asked.

Sienna pulled out her bullet journal and quickly flicked to the right page, reading each one out.

'I've also written a list of people to forgive. I don't know what to do now,' Sienna said.

'Let's pray through each one, using the Bible verses to help us,' Alison said. 'Like this.' She looked at the first verse written in the notebook.

'Dear Jesus,' Alison prayed. 'Thank you that though we've done wrong things so many times, You forgive us every time.'

Sienna repeated Alison's prayer and thought for a moment about some things she'd done wrong that Jesus had forgiven her for. She felt gratefulness bubble up inside her, making her feel strong.

'Jesus, You forgave me, so I choose to forgive...'

Sienna was reminded of the second verse as Alison prayed.

'Jesus, You forgave me,' Sienna repeated. 'So, I choose to forgive Mum's boss for making her work so hard and not letting her spend the weekend with us.' Sienna remembered all the angry feelings she'd had towards her mum's boss. She imagined them like spiky balls in her hands. She pictured herself letting them go, and them flying away. She let gratefulness replace the angry feelings in her heart.

'Can you ask Jesus to bless him?' Alison said, nudging her gently.

Sienna glanced at Alison. 'Do I have to?'

Alison pointed to the last word on the card. Sienna took a deep breath.

'Jesus, please bless Mum's boss. Please bless him in his work, and with his family, but most importantly, please can he come to know You? Amen.'

Sienna was amazed at how much better she felt when she was praying a blessing over him.

'Do we have time to forgive more people?' Sienna asked Alison.

'We have all the time you need.'

Chapter 28

'When will my feelings catch up with my forgiveness?' Sienna asked as they walked back home.

'What do you mean?' asked Alison.

'When I prayed for Mum's boss, I felt peaceful and excited when I blessed him. Those feelings were there straight away. But when I forgave Mum and then Dad, I didn't have the same feelings.'

'How was it different?'

Sienna thought for a moment. 'It's like pushing a buggy or a pram and hitting a bump. You have to push quite hard to get over it. With Mum's boss, the peaceful feelings were there straight away. But when I tried to bless Mum and Dad, it was like there was a bump and it was really difficult.'

'That's because you've been hurt. The big bump is like a bruise inside you.'

'Will it go away, or does it stay forever?'

'It'll take a while, like a bruise on your body takes time to heal. But I know you will keep forgiving, keep blessing them, keep talking to Jesus. One day you'll find it's not such a big bump, it's not *so* difficult to bless them.'

'Will it ever totally go away?'

'I don't know.'

When they reached home, Sienna gave Alison a big hug.

'Do you want to come in?' she asked.

'No, I'm going home to lie down in a dark room.' Alison laughed. 'Your brothers totally wore me out.'

Sienna waved at Alison as she walked down the street. She pushed open the door.

'Hi, I'm home!' she called.

'Can you come up here?' Mum's voice drifted down from her bedroom. Sienna raced up the stairs and popped her head around the door. Mum was sitting in front of her computer.

'You've got an email from your dad,' she said, standing up and holding out the chair for Sienna to sit down. On the screen was an open email. Mum left the room as Sienna started to read.

Dear Sienna,

Thank you so much for the beautiful card. Your mum sent me photographs. I'm so sorry I can't see it for real.

I live and work a long way away, but we can email each other. My contract finishes in eight months, and I don't know what will happen after that.

I work long hours and live in a hotel with other people who have similar jobs.

I must go now. Thank you again for writing to me. I hope you'll email me again.

Take care,

Dad.

Chapter 29

Sienna read the email three or four times before she heard a knock on the door.

'Can I come in?'

Sienna laughed. 'It's your room.'

Mum sat on the bed.

'Are you OK?'

'I'm glad he wrote back. I was worried that he wouldn't. But I don't understand why we didn't write to him before. It's not difficult to do.'

'No, it isn't. But when he left, we were both very angry. We said things we shouldn't have, and we were both wrong. For a long time, we didn't talk or have any contact.' Mum took a deep breath. 'Do you remember, last year, when you read in the Bible that you are special to God, like a treasure, and prayed that you would see others like that?'

Sienna nodded.

'Well,' Mum continued, 'God showed me He saw your dad as a treasure, and I needed to see him as God did.'

'Wow,' Sienna said. 'God sees *Dad* as a treasure too?'

'Yes, I'd never considered that before, and it wasn't easy to change the way I thought,' Mum continued. 'But just before Christmas, I emailed him, and told him I was sorry for the bad things I'd said. I didn't know what he would say, but he wrote back and asked how you all were.'

Sienna wiped away the tears that were falling down her cheeks.

Mum looked in Sienna's eyes.

'I've asked your dad for forgiveness, but I need to say sorry to you too. I'm sorry for being so angry with your dad, and not being open with you about him. I didn't want to speak or think about him, and that was wrong of me. I should've given you the space you needed to ask your questions and talk about him. I'm sorry.'

'I forgive you, Mum,' Sienna said, finding it wasn't as difficult to say now as it had been earlier.

'Jack, Theo, we need a family meeting.' Mum pulled out a chair and sat at the kitchen table.

Jack and Theo tumbled through the door, fighting each other for an action figure. Sienna leaned over and took the character out of Jack's hand and put it on the windowsill.

'Sit down, boys. We've got something very important to tell you.' Mum looked at Sienna and raised her eyebrows. 'Do you remember on Valentine's Day, at Kids' Church, we each made a card for someone?' Sienna asked.

The boys nodded.

'I gave my card to Mummy,' Theo smiled at Mum.

'I made a card for Mrs Smith. When I took it round, she didn't say much.' Jack's smile dissolved into a small frown.

Sienna took a deep breath. 'I made a card for Dad.' Jack and Theo froze. For a moment, no one moved.

'Our dad?' asked Jack. Sienna nodded.

'My dad?' Theo asked, looking at Mum.

'Yes. Your dad, Theo. You've never met him. He works a long way away.'

'So, what happened? Did he get the card? Did he like it?' Jack leaned forward, staring at Sienna.

She glanced at Mum.

'Sort of. It's complicated.'

Jack threw himself back into his chair and folded his arms.

'Now you sound like Mum,' he snapped.

'Yes, he got the card, and he wrote back, saying thank you. You can send him emails or pictures too if you want.'

Jack stood up, making his chair fall over behind him.

'How come Sienna got to write to Dad, and I didn't?' Jack shouted at Mum, before running out of the room

Chapter 30

Sienna was nearly asleep when she heard a noise from the room next door. She got out of bed, pulled on her dressing gown, and went through to the boys' room.

'S'enna!' Theo reached out for her, like he used to do when he was a baby. Sienna glanced at the top bunk and saw a bundle of bedclothes which hid Jack.

Sienna picked Theo up and sat down on the bottom bunk, trying not to bang her head on the top one.

'So, you want to talk?' she asked quietly.

'Yes,' muttered a small voice from the top bunk. 'I've got lots of questions.'

'Me too.' Sienna sighed.

'I've actually written mine down.' Jack lowered himself to the floor and have her a shaky smile. 'Can we start with the simple ones? Where is Dad?'

Sienna put Theo on the bed and walked over to a world map that hung on the boys' wall. She had to look carefully, but she finally found the country she was looking for.

'He's in a country in the Middle East. He's working and has to stay there for eight more months. He can't send letters from there, but he can email.' Sienna pointed to the country and then back to where they lived, to show how far away it was.

'So Mum was right. He really does work a long way away.' Jack said, looking closely at the map.

Sienna moved back to the bed and picked up Theo. After a minute, Jack came over and sat on the bed next to her, leaning on her shoulder slightly. Theo snuggled close, and Sienna blinked back tears.

All three children looked up as Mum came into the room. They hadn't heard her coming up the stairs.

'I thought I heard talking,' she said. 'Are you guys OK?' She knelt in front of them and pulled them all into a big hug.

After a minute, Jack looked up. 'We've got some questions.' Mum nodded. Jack pulled a piece of paper out of his pyjama pocket and straightened it out.

'Question number one, fingers on buzzers,' he announced, staring at the paper.

Mum laughed out loud, but quickly stopped herself when she saw Jack's serious face.

'Can I write to Dad?'

'Yes, of course.' Mum looked like she was going to say more, but Jack interrupted.

'Correct. Question two. Can we see him?'

'If you want to, when he comes back to Britain.'

'Correct. Question three. Will he live here with us?'

'No. He'll have to live near his work.'

'So, he won't work near us?' Jack asked, forgetting his Quiz Master role for a moment.

'We don't know yet. But if he works near here, he'll get his own place nearby,' Mum said.

'Correct. Question four.'

Sienna and Mum glanced at each other and grinned.

'Does he know not to eat duck seed?' Jack looked up. 'That was Theo's question.'

'Duck seed is very owie!' Theo said in a very sleepy voice.

Mum nodded slowly before answering.

'Your dad hasn't been around children or in this country for a long time, so maybe he hasn't fed the ducks in a while. But when he comes back – if he comes back - we can share with him the things we like to do. Maybe he can teach us some new things we haven't done before. It will be like starting a new friendship. It might take a bit of time.'

Mum took a deep breath. 'How about we pray together for your dad?' Jack and Sienna nodded. Theo answered with a tiny snore, which made everyone smile.

'Dear Jesus, thank You for bringing the children's dad back into their lives. We're gonna need Your help because this is a brand-new adventure we've never had before. Please give us Your peace and guide us every step of the way.'

'Jesus, please can Dad like adventures and drawing, and please can he like me,' prayed Jack.

'And please can he come to know You too, because I don't know if he does. Amen,' said Sienna.

Chapter 31

'Happy birthday dear Jack, Happy birthday to you.'

Mum, Sienna and Theo cheered. Jack stood and took a bow, still in his pyjamas.

Mum had made a special breakfast of pancakes, and there were a couple of presents next to Jack's plate.

'I know you are looking forward to your party later today, but we have a special surprise for you now.'

Jack looked eagerly at the gifts. Mum pulled out her mobile phone and after pushing a few buttons, handed it to Jack.

'Your dad has made you a short video message.'

Jack looked at Mum, then down at the screen.

A voice came from the phone, and Jack pulled it closer.

'Hi, Jack. Happy birthday. I can't believe you're eight. Hope you have a great day. Your mum says you're going to have a party. Hope you enjoy it. Take care, and happy birthday. Bye.'

After a moment, Jack pressed the screen, and the message played again. Sienna and Theo crowded close to see the image on the screen.

After watching it a couple more times, Jack handed the phone back to Mum.

'Are you OK?' Mum asked, squeezing Jack's hand. Jack nodded, glancing quickly at the phone.

'Pancakes!' shouted Theo, making everyone laugh. And the birthday breakfast began.

Sienna and Jack carried the last few plates through to the kitchen. Although the party hadn't been the crazy experience Jack had planned, everyone had enjoyed themselves. Jack's friends had been generous with their gifts, and they'd all joined in the party games Sienna had invented. Now, the last person had gone home, and Mum was upstairs giving Theo a bath.

'Did Dad look like you remembered?' asked Jack, throwing a dirty napkin into the bin.

'He looked older, and he was wearing glasses, but I think he looked the same. It's hard to see on the phone.'

Jack tilted his head on one side.

'I don't remember Dad very well, but he looked like I *imagined* Dad looked, so that's good. After seeing him in the video message, I want to see him again. It's going to be a long wait till he comes back.'

'Yes, and he works really hard. Mum was up half the night waiting for him to send the video. In the end he had to pretend he was going to the toilet to record it – that's why it was so short.'

'He messaged me from the toilet?' Jack pulled a face, making Sienna laugh.

'No, I think it was just a corridor!'

Jack paused for a moment.

'Sienna, do you really think he'll come back?'

'I hope so, but it's still a long way away, Jack. I'm sure we'll have more adventures while we are waiting!'

And Sienna was right. A new adventure was just around the corner.

Some questions for you

As you've read the book, you might be asking questions. So, here's an opportunity for you to think a bit more about the story.

Chapter 1

Sienna lives with her mum and little brothers. One day, as she is eating dinner, Sienna feels a 'niggle' – a little thought that something is not quite right. She knows this can be God giving her an idea. Does God sometimes give you good ideas? You can find out more about how God talks to Sienna in *The Treasure Man*.

Chapter 2

Sienna is angry with her mum's boss. It's not wrong to be angry. But for Sienna, these angry feelings grow into nasty thoughts. Alison called it being bitter. Sometimes, if we don't talk about our angry feelings, they can grow. Do you have a parent or older friend you can talk to when you get angry?

Chapter 3

Jack's birthday has sad memories for him and Sienna. They are very brave to share that sadness with Alison. Sometimes it's hard to talk about things that make us sad, but it is important. Why is it good to talk about our sad feelings?

Chapter 4

Sienna enjoys thinking of ideas to help Mum, but she isn't too impressed when Alison adds her own thoughts. How do you feel when someone else has an idea that is very different to yours?

Chapter 5

Alison hasn't fed the ducks in a long time and doesn't know she has to buy duck seed. Sometimes grown-ups don't know how things have changed. Sienna and Jack try to explain politely. Have you had to explain something to a grown-up? Was it difficult?

Chapter 6

Do you like Valentine's Day? Why / Why not? What do you think about Sienna's idea of thanking the important people in your life? Is this something you might think of doing?

Chapter 7

Sienna now feels angry towards God. Because Mum has to work so hard, she questions whether God really cares for them. This question pops up often in our lives. But the Bible tells us that God does care. Alison reads about that in Matthew 6:25-26 We need to choose whether to trust the Bible or our feelings. This is difficult, isn't it?

Chapter 8

Lots of people find journaling useful. Do you have a notebook where you can write your questions to God and His answers to you? Did you know there is a 'Love From Sienna' Journal – just like the one Sienna uses?

Chapter 9

Sienna finds out that maybe her plans aren't as good as she first thought. Mrs Khan and Emily both give her different perspectives. Have you ever found out that your ideas and plans weren't as great as you first thought?

Chapter 10

Mum says that grace is God forgiving us, even when we don't deserve it. Because Mum knows God has forgiven her, she can forgive someone else. Jesus told a story about it in the Bible. You can find it in Matthew 18:21-35. Have you heard this story before?

Chapter 11

Sienna has some hard questions to ask God, so she writes them in the journal. It's OK to have big questions for God. Sienna finds it easier to write her questions down. Other people prefer to just ask God their questions. What do you find easier?

Chapter 12

Sienna suggests that Emily talks to Sophia. Sophia is in a similar situation with her mum also expecting a baby. Sometimes it helps if you have a friend who is going through the same thing in life. Can you think of a time a friend helped you (or you helped a friend) because you were both going through the same thing?

Chapter 13

Saying 'thank you' changes our hearts and helps us see difficult things in a new way. Instead of looking at the problems, Sienna starts with little 'thank you's. Soon she is able to see more things to be thankful for. Can you try to find something to be thankful for, even when life is difficult?

Chapter 14

Sienna and her mum are doing chores together. They use the time to talk and catch up. Do you enjoy doing chores with your family? Have you tried talking or playing music together to make the work more fun?

Chapter 15

Jack wants to create an amazing surprise for his family, but no one is happy about it. Mum is angry. Have you ever tried to do something nice for someone – but they didn't think it was good?

Chapter 16

Theo is hurt and Jack thinks it's his fault. It was his idea to recreate the duck pond, and now Theo is in pain. Jack feels terrible. Mum tells Jack it isn't his fault. What could you say to help Jack?

Chapter 17

Sienna and Jack don't know what to do – so they pray. They ask Mrs Smith to pray too, although she hasn't prayed for a very long time – not since she was a little girl. Do you find it easy to pray with people? Some people do, some don't.

Chapter 18

Sienna's dad disappeared from their lives four years ago. Whenever Sienna asked, Mum said Dad was working away and Sienna was too little to understand. Sienna thinks about her dad a lot, but doesn't talk to Mum about him any more. Now Sienna hears her mum talking about contacting her dad. How do you think she feels?

Chapter 19

Sienna and her mum talk all the time, but they have avoided talking about certain things. Those subjects are painful for them. Now Sienna and her mum need to work hard at listening to each other and talking about these difficult subjects. Do you sometimes find it hard to talk about things that hurt you?

Chapter 20

'The greatest love was given to us when we least deserved it. That is grace – God's forgiveness and love to us, when we are at our worst.' Do you know this love? Maybe you don't know Jesus like Sienna and Jack do. If you want to know Jesus better, you can start with a simple prayer, like this one:

Dear Jesus, Thank You for loving me when I didn't deserve it. I want to know you more. Please help me. Amen.

Chapter 21

Sienna doesn't know if her dad knows Jesus, so she wrote and told him she is praying for him. She also wrote a verse from the Bible. Do you have a favourite verse in the Bible? Can you practise using this verse to tell someone about why you believe in Jesus, so you are always ready if someone asks you?

Chapter 22

In some countries in the world, it is illegal to be a Christian, and when people believe in Jesus, they must keep it a secret. Why not take a moment to pray for your Christian brothers and sisters who live in these countries?

Dear Jesus, I pray for my brothers and sisters who live in these countries. I especially pray for children my age. Please protect them and keep them close to You. May they know You are their best friend, even when everything is very difficult. Amen.

Chapter 23

Mum asks God to help her when she is talking to her boss. Suddenly, in her mind, she sees a picture. God can use pictures to speak to us. Did you know you can ask God for help at any time? You don't have to pray out loud. You can think a little prayer, like this:

Jesus, please help me. I don't know what to do or say!

Chapter 24

Mrs Smith's dad struggled with his mental health. Back then, no one really knew how to help, but now we know much more. The first step is always finding a safe person to talk to, whether that is someone in your family, your school or your church. Being able to talk about how you feel is very important. Do you have someone you can talk to?

Chapter 25

God has forgiven us of all the wrong things we have said or done. Because of that forgiveness, we can forgive other people. We show we have no anger left in our hearts by blessing them. This isn't easy – that's why we need Jesus to help us. Is there anyone you need to forgive? (Remember, Jack had to forgive himself!)

Chapter 26

These are enormous issues. They are not easy for Sienna, or us, to learn. Mum says, 'Sometimes the anger is very deep, or the hurt continues, and you need to forgive again and again. Sometimes lots of times. But we are always asking Jesus to help us forgive and remembering how much He forgave us.' Are these words helpful to you?

Chapter 27

Can you use these prayers to help you forgive people? Think about the words like Sienna did.

'Dear Jesus, thank You for forgiving me every time I do or say something wrong.'

'Jesus, You forgave me, so I choose to forgive [name the person]*'*

'Please bless [name the person]*'.* Can you pray a special blessing over them?

Chapter 28

Alison talked about forgiving people even when it hurts. Sometimes those angry feeling stay for a while. It's hard work to keep forgiving. But talking to Jesus, and thanking Him for His love and forgiveness, helps us in those tough times. Do you find it easy to keep talking to Jesus, or sometimes, is it hard?

Chapter 29

Sienna's mum had made a mistake by not telling Sienna more about her dad. She doesn't want to make the same mistake with Jack and Theo. Can you think of a time you learned from a mistake and did something better?

Chapter 30

Life will be different if Sienna's dad comes back. Maybe it won't be easy! It's always a good idea to pray and ask for Jesus' help in new situations and new friendships. Is there anything you want to ask God about now?

Chapter 31

Sienna and Jack will have to wait awhile until they meet their dad in person. It's hard to wait sometimes, isn't it? Do you want to hear more about their adventures?

More books by Joy Vee

 Sienna has never noticed the homeless man near her house, until she begins to understand how previous we all are to God. With her eyes opened, she and her younger brothers, together with their mum, seek to strike up a friendship with this 'treasure man'.
ISBN: 978-1-912-72637-0

 Sienna is on a Mission. Her mum has to work long hours for an unfair boss, and Sienna is determined to make her life easier. Despite all her careful planning, none of her ideas work out as she hoped. As Sienna learns to listen to God through reading the Bible and Journaling, she begins to see the world differently.
ISBN: 978-1-915-03401-4

 The 'Love From Sienna' Journal teaches and encourages fans of Sienna to go deeper into Scripture. With Bible verses, inspirational quotes and blank pages, this bullet journal is a perfect first step. Spiral Bound. Only available from Joyvee.org/shop
ISBN: 978-1-915034-10-6

Acknowledgements

Thank you to Jesus – without whom there would be no story!

Thank you to my family, Andriy, Michael and Anna for doing so much cooking and cleaning while I've been busy. A special shout-out to Anna for all the help with everything creative. Thank you for helping me get my words into picture form.

Thank you to Sheila Jacobs for her amazing editing and advice throughout this project. You help me be a better writer.

A huge thank you to Alex Taylor for bringing his tremendous design talents to the project and giving us such an amazing cover. Your creativity and professionalism have blown me away.

To my Wednesday Zoom girls, Sienna, Lily, Acacia, Isabella, Lois and Tally. I so enjoy spending Wednesday afternoons with you. Thank you for telling me when bits were rubbish or too hard to understand. I hope we can keep talking, dreaming and inspiring each other.

To Natalie Coles and Lockhart Geddes for reading and giving your invaluable feedback. You have helped make the messages shine.

To my proof readers, Catherine L. Owen, Barbara Downie and Mark Hinde for picking up my many errors.

Big hugs to everyone who inspired me on this writing journey, especially Auntie Shirley, Joy Gillespie, Caroline Johnson, Joy Margetts and Karen Rosario Ingerslev.

To my extended family, especially Mum and Dad, the Nordens, the Keels, the Rogers, the Meighs, and the Velykorodnyys. Our zoom calls have been my sanity over the last year. Can't wait till we can hug again!

Finally, to everyone who loved Sienna and the Treasure Man. Thank you for all your reviews, encouragements, emails, testimonies and for that question 'Is there a sequel?' Yes! Here it is. I hope you enjoy it. Please stay in touch by signing up to my newsletter at joyvee.org.

About the Author

Joy Vee lives in Motherwell, Scotland with her husband. She is the mother of two teenage children who have huge dreams.

When Joy was 23, she moved to Ukraine, where she lived for 5 years before meeting the man she was going to marry. Her writing skills were developed in her newsletters throughout those early years of email. However, they were then put on the back burner as children and family life took over.

Joy's first published book, The Treasure Man, was written as a Christmas present to her niece. It launched her on a publishing and writing journey she'd always dreamed of but never really imagined possible. Using her nephews and nieces as inspiration, the 'Sienna' series, starting with The Treasure Man, is aimed at 7–11-year-olds. The soon-to-be published 'Kai' series will be for 6–9-year-olds.

To buy Joy's books or contact her, check out her website, www.joyvee.org. Make sure you sign up for the newsletter for special offers and news.

Coming soon

KAI

Lightning Source UK Ltd.
Milton Keynes UK
UKHW010059030921
389898UK00002B/128